WOOD FOR THE TREES

A novel by
Ian Belshaw

Printed in Australia

First Printing: October 2020

Shawline Publishing Group Pty Ltd
www.shawlinepublishing.com.au

Paperback - ISBN- 9781922444011

Ebook - ISBN- 9781922444028

Ian Belshaw was born in Sydney, Australia.

A longtime songwriter, lyricist and musician, he holds a deep fascination with language and an interest in Australian history.

Ian currently lives in Melbourne with his partner Kristen and their cat Jinx.

'Wood For The Trees' is his first novel.

To Kristen,
Like fire on a raging sea.

While acknowledging the men and women in whose sweat and blood this nation was born, the author also wishes to acknowledge those who inhabited the land we call Australia for millennia before.

WOOD FOR THE
TREES

Ian Belshaw

- CHAPTER 1 -

Luke had always dreamed of being a bushranger. A steady diet of bush yarns had coloured his youth with a romantic view of the past that only burgeoned with time. The wide, open spaces, frontier living, dusty trails and spirit of adventure lured him with a magnetic pull impossible to resist. These were days of real men: gritty and raw, flawed, yet fighting for survival in an unfamiliar world. Their names were starbursts of light in deepest night: the Kelly Gang and their enigma of iron; Gentleman Ben Hall, who never pulled a trigger; Frank Gardiner, the King of the Road; Captains Thunderbolt, Melville, Moonlite... Their deeds and mythology blended as one. They took on the status of colonial gods, imbued with limitless courage, upholding true justice in the face of unfair might. Their fast burning flames and ne'er forgotten names were everything Luke wanted. Theirs were lives freed of mundanity, worthy sacrifices for freedom's glorious cause. To what more could a man possibly aspire?

Schooling came and went, with the Humanities alone keeping his attention. Even then, it was only the occasional flash of local history, Australian geography or patriotic literature that held him enthralled. He preferred to spend his hours in libraries or open air, reading of his heroes' exploits and then preparing to emulate them, all to a soundtrack of folk songs of yore.

With neither horses nor guns readily available, he focused for the time being on other aspects of a bushman's craft: from starting campfires, to cooking damper, to learning about edible native fruits, and taking baby steps into hunting, skinning and gutting.

When possible, Luke would load his swag and sneak away for the night, immersing himself in bush that felt removed from suburbia, even if it wasn't. He'd practise his skills and set his wits against the elements, aware that these would challenge an outlaw as much as the authorities.

Once freed of the classroom, he worked odd jobs, bringing in cash to fund the overarching goal. His parents found him a studious young man, and he was rarely less than respectful. They thought his interests quaint, though harmless, and bound to dissipate once the lures of women and partying inevitably took over. He never badgered his parents for driving lessons and made his own way as well as he could. Independence was encouraged, but there remained a strong bond of parental concern, ready to tighten and protect when required. As Luke grew out of his teenage years, any reliance decreased, and his parents chose acceptance instead of pursuit. Their son was his own man now and the world was ripe to take. Concern would never waver, but to pry would be wrong.

He was blind to the subtext of female advances and far too uncouth to make moves of his own, yet he dreamed deep of maidens in practical dresses, their hair flowing long and their skin fresh as snow. He saw them through the prism of colonial times; faithful and proper, yet spirited and proud. Far enough removed from wild convict roots to know their place yet still too free spirited to ever be tamed. Luke idealised these images that life to date had failed to flesh out. Even if it had, he was ill-prepared to act. He merely assumed that fate would take charge, that where his own skills were lacking and could never be honed, there'd be a hand of intervention to make things right.

His excursions away increased in both frequency and length. From time to time a curious friend (for he was not completely friendless) would tag along, though his level of self-sufficiency would often leave them ill-prepared. He travelled light and tested himself in hard conditions, often emerging from the bush rain-drenched and starving. With money earned, he paid for riding lessons, which supplemented his extensive reading on horse-craft and his command of equine terminology. He purchased replica pistols and felt his hands become one with their shape, their feel and their texture. No western gunslinger, his weapons were discreet and his visage distinctly Australian. He joined a local gun club to learn how to shoot, finding a natural aptitude with these modern barrels of metal. Each target in sights was a trap or a traitor; each successful hit a strike for freedom.

Where others saw such undertakings as hobbies or interests, to Luke they were another step on the path of his destiny. In no way did his inspiration sour with time. The enjoyment he found in these rustic pursuits was vindication of the life he had chosen. To be one with the bush and live the life of his childhood idols.

To Luke's way of thinking, the lusts and demands of global connectivity had buried the bedrock from which this nation birthed. The values of mateship, the shirt off one's back, the sweat stains of toil and yarns told at day's end had faded from view. The rich were becoming richer, the poor poorer and the stakes ever higher. The highwaymen and stick-up merchants now wore suits of silk instead of suits of steel, fleecing their victims down loaded barrels of fine print and leaving them for dead. It was a cut-throat world. It always had been. Only now the methods seemed more underhanded and faceless. Where an old-school outlaw would seek safety in the forest and the loyalty of kin, refuge was now in the anonymity of cyberspace, the shelter of wealth and the tight-knit bonds of the business elite. Where once you could see your assailant, could smell his breath, could stare down the whites of his eyes, now you were surrounded by an unknown and merciless force. This was a world created by man, not evolved with the ages. For those lost in its cynical churn or who felt no genuine connection, the rawer struggles of earlier times were a symbol of how things could still be.

Luke drifted further and further from regular life, seeing anything but essential diversions as a waste of his precious time. Bushrangers lived fast and died young. The likes of Flash Johnny Gilbert and Bold Jack Donohue thrived on the energy and impetuosity of youth. A middle-aged bushranger was one who was no good.

A sense of urgency therefore characterised his behaviour, with frustration close at hand when speed bumps rose in the way. A nasty case of pneumonia left him restless. The loss of a job left him desperately scrounging for funds for his continued development. In true highwayman style, he could have stolen money to survive, but he wasn't ready for that just yet. The irony was that most of his idols weren't ready for it either; the cruel hand of fate drove them to their profession. On Luke, entitled and comfortable, this irony was lost.

Romance aside, there was a criminal aspect to this career choice. This was not something Luke was necessarily drawn to, but he'd long since come to terms with the fact that a bushranger who didn't commit robbery under arms would never really be a bushranger at all. Perhaps, with a sharper imagination, he may have followed his idols' principles in a broader or more figurative sense. Instead, spurred to faithful re-enactment with minimal modern twists, he took to planning a way to add his own name to the history books.

With several reference points and varying styles, his plan of attack fluctuated with time. The callous barbarity of Mad Dan Morgan neither appealed to nor suited him, while he knew he would struggle to construct a true outlaw 'gang' in the Kelly or Gardiner moulds. His method would be an amalgam of many, leaning most heavily on the 'gentleman bushranger' persona. His gains would be shared, and consistent with tobymen of lore he would hold court in pubs and bars, shouting round after round from the depths of his benevolence. Women would swoon, men would fume, and old balladeers would croon. He'd defy the law with a glint in his eye and a cry for the common man. And then he'd ride off into the night, elusive and lethal, to slumber in silence until surfacing again. He'd lead those traps a merry dance. 'Who knows,' he mused, 'they may even bring back the Felons Act and public hanging before I'm done'.

Planning was meticulous and if he was aware of little else, he knew full well that times had changed and there would be many obstacles in his way. Gone were the days of inept, poorly equipped troopers, loyal bush telegraphs and vast tracts of rugged and unfenced land. There were no longer gold escorts to hold up and the way of a traveller in a metal projectile at eighty miles an hour was difficult to block. Yet he had read enough recent history to know that absconded convicts and wanted felons had been known to elude capture for extended periods, protected by the countryside and subsisting as best they could off the land and its tenants. Many of the haunts favoured by bushrangers were in isolated terrain. If well-prepared, resilient, and game, there was no reason he couldn't go down in history a true descendant of the nation's folk villains.

One concession to modernity related to the procurement of firearms. Common sense dictated that he would need to break character. There was not much future in raising a nineteenth century weapon against modern artillery. He still had his replica pistols for historical effect, but for the nitty gritty of his endeavours he'd need something with more grunt. And he wanted people to fear him rather than laugh at an ornate choice of handgun. No point putting himself in unnecessary danger; he planned his spree to last a year or two, rather than to send him immediately into oblivion. Through contacts in the gun club he sourced the pieces for the task, steering clear of semi-automatics in deference to traditional tools. He took them on his increasingly frequent bush missions, shooting random objects with unerring accuracy and growing pride. He felt ready. He felt in control. He felt as though he was on the verge of greatness.

Luke set the date. 15 June was his chosen moment, marking the anniversary of the largest heist in bushranging history. He quit his job and made final arrangements, though there was little more to organise. It was more a matter of shifting the balance of intention from future to present. After such a protracted build-up this took some effort, though he steeled himself and readied for action with the assurance that this was his purpose, his calling, his fate. He loaded his swag with non-perishable sustenance, basic tools and what little money he had left. There was no need to withdraw from any bank; as someone destined to hold them up, why would he have ever trusted their shaky vaults? He would rely on his wits and the bedrock of his skills. True, he would also rely on surprise and the strength of his firepower, though he knew neither would protect him long in the wild. Even a dingo needs more tricks than just his teeth.

Dawn on 15 June was crisp as a new season apple. When the morning sun rose over his parents' cream-brick home, Luke was long-risen and nearly as long gone. Bags packed the night before, he had dressed after fitful sleep, concealed his weapons and snuck into the darkness. He felt a new man, as though life started now, and the scribes of great deeds should stand to attention. He'd dressed like a bushman, with a touch of flashiness – Johnny Gilbert style – though not fancily enough to draw attention so soon in the piece.

He carried his swag and walked with steady gait towards the local train station, where he boarded the first westbound train of the day. The train was virtually empty and the few people who shared his carriage did not share his alertness. As stations came and stations went, he relaxed somewhat into the character he was to become.

Patience would be a vital companion, as it always had been. And while his blood was running hot, there was no point boiling over before he had something to get excited about. For now, it was a matter of staying calm and sticking to procedure.

At the outer reaches of suburbia, he alighted the train and waited for the next: the one that would take him across the threshold. Bleary-eyed commuters filed onto the opposite platform: modern-day office workers naïve to all but their own prism of existence. Staring blankly into space or playing with their mobile phones, they were worlds away from him. Automatons in human form. They were also the working-class rabble he could inspire by his actions. The potential sympathisers and harbourers of a man who was fighting an unjust system, a world gone rotten, a place out of time. They were the excitement-starved masses, either shunned or victimised by authority, who would be drawn to the romance of his tale, just as he was drawn to the tales of those before. The difference for them was that they would experience it in real time, fed by the almost instantaneous flow of the twenty-first century news cycle. This would be uncommon magic in a pedestrian world: a break from the drollery of social media, reality television and cat videos. The masses were in for a treat. They just didn't know it yet.

His next and final train arrived. Then, as a commuter of a different kind, he leaned back on a creaking seat and continued to a place where his talents might soon be employed.

It was mid-morning by the time he arrived in Bathurst, in the glorious old gold-belt of colonial New South Wales.

This had been John Peisley's turf, prime bushranging land, stained deep with frontier blood and sewn with bullets from skirmishes of yore. As the largest town west of the divide, Luke saw Bathurst as an appropriate launching pad. Anywhere smaller and he'd struggle to find whatever supplies he might need, and he'd stand out more than he already did. He wanted attention, but not until fair cause had been given for it to come his way.

Not wanting notice ran against his original intention to travel on horseback. As faithful as he wanted to remain to tradition, he had already compromised on weaponry and similarly relented with transportation. Not to say that he wouldn't seek to ride from time to time. It just meant he couldn't exactly trot on farrier's wares down the Midwestern Highway. Where he could keep faith with tradition, however, was in his procurement of a mode of carriage. Wandering quiet backstreets away from the heart of Bathurst Town, he found four wheels instead of legs and took ownership in the same unlawful way as his heroes acquired horseflesh.

Despite having never formally learnt to drive, he had determined how to jimmy open a car door and hot-wire an engine. He also proved to have a decent eye for an easy target, with no alarm set and no enraged owner following his haphazard virgin path down a drowsy, tree-lined street. No master of his craft, he gingerly manoeuvred this unfamiliar beast around similarly unfamiliar streets, avoiding collisions and gradually building a degree of misplaced confidence. In the moment's excitement, it took a while to realise that he had committed his first crime. Short of returning stolen goods in shame-faced contrition, there truly was no turning back now.

Aware that a missing vehicle could quickly stir local suspicion, but also aware that he'd soon need fuel, he took the road out of Bathurst and found the first available petrol station. Hands shaking more than expected, Luke filled the petrol tank and a large jerry can with gushing jets of fuel. He felt a little shifty when dealing with the attendant, watching for signs of alarm, even though he knew any reports of theft would take time to filter down the line. Apart from that, he continued to do all he could to look normal and at ease.

Later that day, in gloaming reflection, cooking damper on a fire in the bracing winter cold, he realised he didn't really care if he was recognised or not. The aim was to be notorious and renowned, yet untouchable, rather than to subsist in the shadows.

On rolling wheels over rolling plains, he journeyed south west into the Lachlan Valley. The towns he passed were the siren calls of his youth: Carcoar, Canowindra, Eugowra. Eulogised hovels bitten cruel by the ravages of time. They flickered with remnant flames of olden charm that provided warmth and steeled resolve. He could tame these lands. Sleepy backwaters filled with feckless souls: hardly razor-edge propellants to future glories. Their glories were gone, dried up when the gold ran out. History was all that sustained them, along with the tenuous gifts of browned and paper-dry land. He'd surely not chosen the most affluent of locales. But to him it was a starting point: a logical, low-risk stake in the ground from which to fan out.

The sun, battered by piercing wintry winds, quickly sunk in the leaden sky. He had travelled as far as he needed and found a secluded campsite by a creek where he could settle in for the night. He longed for past times of open spaces and unfenced paddocks, but he was determined to find whatever tracts of wilderness he might use as cover.

He hid the stolen car as best he could, a safe distance from the campsite, aware that he was unlikely to be tracked but wary lest the stolen car had aroused suspicion. Rugged up and bristling with cold, he struck up a small fire and warmed his quaking bones. He seared a steak on a grill above the flames, taking this chance to eat well before stooping to canned or dehydrated fare.

He listened to the sounds of the bush and the crackling of fire, feeling at home and not the slightest bit lonely. Well-fed and exhausted, more mentally than physically, he unfurled his swag, smothered the coals and drifted away into the night.

- CHAPTER 2 -

Stephen Owens had never dreamed of being a bushranger. Not even once. It was not that he lacked imagination; he just focused on the modern world and more prosaic aspects of existence.

He also never dreamed of becoming a police officer, but that is what he became. Now, after twenty years in the force, he was a Senior Sergeant of no small renown, awarded and heralded throughout the Central West.

He wore bravery as his crest and was strident in his commitment to the local community. His was not a crusade to rid the area of crime per se; it was more a matter of doing the job as best he could and of not letting anyone down. It saw him rest easy most nights, despite the stresses interwoven with his choice of career. There were moments of doubt and times when he questioned his judgment, but he always had training and faith to fall back on.

Senior Sergeant Owens had a hook next to the front door of his house and he always left his hat there upon coming home. It was a symbolic detachment from the day he'd had and a commitment that the hours ahead were dedicated to family, no matter what had come before.

It didn't always pan out that way, but his doting wife was quick to pull him up if he slipped into detail about the day's travails. He needed an outlet, as well she knew, but that outlet needed to be somewhere beyond these four walls. Their youngest had recently started high school and was reaching a tricky, volatile age. The middle child was two years advanced, with the scent of a rebel on her newly perfumed skin. The eldest was, at fifteen, convinced he was already a man. With little aptitude for school he was obsessed with machinery, his fingers all cables and cotters and pulleys and pistons, his mind a tool to create and pull apart. Yet, for all the growing pains and familial strains, they were resourceful children dipping toes in the waters of a tremulous world.

His wife was by turns stone and sand, supporting and giving in equal measure. She was a voice of reason when his methods were in doubt, and a reliable foil when he needed it most. And if she was tempestuous from time to time, which she surely was, it was never through lack of affection. He knew he wasn't always the easiest to deal with, hence the rule to leave war stories at the door. Meditation and prayer, along with the occasional chat to a colleague, were his cleansing apparatuses. Hours spent with those closest to him added much needed balm and poultice.

In his years of service, Owens had had his fair share of dealings with the nefarious. Armed robbery, murder, rape, child abuse, large-scale drug dealing, and violent assaults. He'd knocked on countless doors, provoking torrents of grief, disbelieving glares and frantic efforts to escape. He preferred to 'take the bullet' in these situations than to throw a green recruit to the wolves.

Sometimes he knew the faces he saw and recalled an innocence never to be seen again. These were the grim realities of his calling, and they never failed to cut to the bone. It could be said that he grew colder with time, though it could also be said that he simply coped. Even so, no amount of bodies broken, or lives destroyed, could truly prepare him for his next horrific encounter.

After twenty years he was wearied, though there was still a spark within. He figured he had another two decades in him before pulling up stumps and finding a less arduous way to pass the time. With their offspring growing and having formed something of a pubescent cabal, both Owens and his wife were now working full-time. The extra money was a godsend and while it shifted the domestic dynamic, his wife's increased workload had done her independence a world of good. There were still times when a tangled criminal web would ensnare the veteran policeman, dragging him away for extended periods of time, but these were less frequent than on the proving ground of his fresh-faced years. By fortune or foresight, balance had been found. Or so it would seem.

On the evening of 15 June, Senior Sergeant Owens was ensconced in the family abode, warming aching limbs by a crackling fire. His wife had joined him in the living room, she on one couch, he on the other. The kids were in their rooms, doing homework, as far as he knew.

An auburn glow infused their bodies as they basked in the remains of the day, concerns set to one side and all troubles faded into inconsequence. The day at the station had been procedural and dry: not what he got into the job for but not what he'd leave it for either. There had been a steady flow of crime in recent times, hammering away at local resources but without stretching them to break. The youth were restless and desperate, which he understood, though he would never understand the steps they'd take to escape the malaise. He hoped his own kids would never feel the need to stoop so low, but he had faith that he and his wife were doing enough to ensure that the flush of teenage rebellion was a passing phase and not propulsion to crime. While he could enact his job by the letter of the law, the ways of his family were anything but black and white.

- CHAPTER 3 -

'Can I help you, sir?'

'Sum cunt stole me wheels.'

'The wheels of your car?'

'Yeah. Took the whole thing.'

'Okay. I will need a few details from you so that we can lodge a report. When did you last see the car?'

'Musta been around midday yesterday. I went 'round to Daryl's for a bit of a session just after then and I'm sure it was parked on the street when I left. Come home this morning and sum cunt has taken it.'

'Okay. And what do you mean by 'session'?'

'You know, got on the cans, that sort of thing. Daryl just did up his man cave and we gave it a bit of a breaking in, you know.'

'So, you came home this morning at roughly what time?'

'Woulda been about 30 minutes ago I reckon.'

'So, around 10 am?'

'Yeah, 'bout that.'

'And were you still intoxicated when you arrived home? It sounds like you had a pretty solid session.'

'Fucken oath I was. But, pissed or not, a man knows when his car's not out the front of his house. And the missus is sober as a nun and she swears blind it's gone as well.'

'That's fine. So, as far as we know, the car has gone missing sometime between 12 pm yesterday and 10 am this morning?'

'No shit, Sherlock.'

'What make and model car are we looking for?'

'She's a 2005 Toyota Camry, silver.'

'And the rego?'

'Ah, BK56LP. Yellow plates, black writing – you know, true New South Wales plates. Premier State'

'Sure. And the address it was last seen at?'

'Me own fucken house. 42 Brown Street, West Bathurst.'

'Thank you, sir.'

'I don't have much hope that you cunts will find it. Couldn't catch AIDS in Africa, you lot.'

'Trust me, sir, we'll do all we can.'

'Heard that before. Better off lookin' meself. Anyway, I've wasted enough of my time for one day.'

Charmed, the operator typed up the details and lodged a report of a missing car, last seen at the front of a West Bathurst dwelling, either stolen or misplaced by a drunk and foul-mouthed bogan.

Sleep, like a faithless friend, invariably lets a man down when needed most.

It also strays in excitement's thrall, unable to resist the churning thrill of anticipation. Luke woke hag-ridden and unrested, his head throbbing and a dull winter sun only making him feel worse. He prepared a billy of tea that he hoped would revitalise and considered returning to his swag when that panacea failed to work. He was his own master now, and while his ambitions were grand, one day here or there was hardly the end of the world. He listened to bird calls: magpies and kookaburras. Sirens of the scrub. He cooked two hard-boiled eggs and sat pensive in a quiet repast. Taken in isolation, this was an idyllic scene. Apart from modern concessions, it was very much the way a bush renegade of yore might have started his day: a man alone but for the breadth of his surrounds and not knowing where he'd be this time tomorrow.

A branch cracked. Not far away. His heart jumped, but he kept composure. Resisting the urge to reach for a gun, he rose and surveyed the scene. He thought it unlikely he was being followed or tracked, but it wouldn't hurt to check, and it was good practice to be on alert. Tiptoeing through tinder-dry leaves, he moved in the direction from which the sound had come. No further sounds came, save those self-created, and his nerves gradually settled again. The branch in question—or a reasonable mimic—came into view. It bore all the signs of death and of having been separated from its mother tree to rot in the undergrowth. As the falseness of the alarm quickly sunk in, he realised that this was an unavoidable aspect of his new existence. Coming to terms with the sounds of nature was one thing – he had long felt at one with the wild—but to be a man hunted was something else entirely. He'd be sleeping with one eye open and the other barely shut.

Camp loaded in the boot of his car, he wound a way out of his creek-bound fort and back into view of the world. He kept to back roads as much as possible, loathe to draw attention, but also eager to familiarise himself with the undulations and modulations of this ancient land.

Landmarks were noted, and distances registered, closely tracing the rutted grooves that gave this country its voice. Some of it he had learnt in advance, but for the rest this was a crash course in local geography, and they were studies that could prove vital in the days, weeks and months ahead.

Senses finely attuned, he was a thirsty student with a savant's mind. He took careful notes in a tattered leather journal, but most of this learning stuck fast in his mind. While there was no way of knowing every ebb and flow of land spanning countless horizons, he intuitively knew what he thought to be the most useful routes and deviations. The skills of a lifetime would do the rest. And the urgent force of necessity would fill any gaps that might be found.

Carving a parabola from his cast-off point, he spent the bulk of the day absorbed in educative endeavours. Luke limited human interaction to a service station visit, where he was careful to obscure the plates of his stolen car from any curious cameras. He didn't know how careful he needed to be, so he naturally tended to more cautious, rather than less. With a seed of action already sown in his mind, he happened upon an outlying property with a crowded paddock of cars. He snuck through a gap in a haggard fence and having settled on a target, approached with measured steps. As hounds whimpered from an unknown distance, his nervous hands turned rusted screws and caught a set of dust-worn plates before they fell to earth. The dogs were still at a distance. Replacing the labels of his dishonour, he immediately felt a slight relief. He was covering his steps and potentially buying more time. The heat would come later once stakes had been raised.

Following the Lachlan River and then veering south, he crept up on the fabled Weddin Mountains. Their crests were less austere than he expected, but the beetling crags of history towered like monoliths against the sky. Hideouts, treasure, and vantage points: this was a boy's own cornucopia of bushranging lore. He'd dreamt of unearthing remains of Frank 'Darkie' Gardiner's gold, stashed around the countryside like morsels stored for winter. He'd had visions of standing atop a giant boulder and taunting the desperate traps below. He'd seen himself perched as an eagle above the plains, free to descend at will and unleash the brunt of his reign. Any stab of disappointment that he might have felt at the insipidness of the scene and lack of montane majesty was but a minor blow.

This dense blanket of trees had eavesdropped on the surreptitious plotting of rogues and had borne witness to escapades of the most daring kind. Apart from – and because of – the declaration of the area as a National Park, he expected that very little had changed since history was first written. Even the ancient custodians of these lands would likely recognise its modern syncopation. This place was not alone in its timeless distinction; his travels around New South Wales had already seen him face to face with such prehistoric wilderness. It delighted him and incited even greater yearning for the days of yore. Days when his ancestors were not only seas away from this land but could never have countenanced their flesh and blood one day pulsing on its shores. As a youth, one generation removed from foundries and farms of the British Isles, he had craved a drop of colonial heredity. As a grown man, he sought to transfuse it into his veins.

A night in the Weddins had always been a part of his plan, as much in homage to the past as to scope out places of future sanctuary. He parked his car a reasonable distance from the road, unloaded supplies and continued, on foot, into the heart of the mountains. After a day behind the wheel it was a relief to stride out, smelling the callow fragrance of the bush and feeling the jab of winter's sting. The colder season and remote locale kept walkers to a minimum, though he had little present fear of passers-by. He gave a friendly wave to those whose path intersected his. With campsites in the vicinity, there was nothing unusual about a man with a swag. Besides, his only crime to date was minor and the scene a distant speck beyond the eastern horizon. He felt safe here, as though renegade spirits drew him to their core, offering shelter and supporting his ambition. As he hiked deeper into the heart of this terrain, he could picture horses being led cautiously across it, scrambling and clambering to sturdy ground.

Their sweat and strain nourished the soil beneath his feet. Yet for all the romance of life in the saddle, he was grateful for the agility of exploring on foot.

Soon enough he came to an overhang sign posted to be Ben Hall's cave. Divorced from its history, there was nothing remarkable about it whatsoever. However, for one so immersed in the viscid slough of legends, it wasn't hard to place himself a century and a half back in time, in the shoes of his idols, when bushrangers' names were on the lips of even the most taciturn members of society. To feel hunted and harried, unsure of friend or foe, with no choice but to carry on, hoping that your wits were enough to get by. This was the life he sought and sitting here in the last rays of the sun, in a mood of solemn obeisance and reflection, thoughts of his hero's travails were the final spur to action. No, he hadn't seen his wife take off with a policeman lover, nor had he seen his possessions burn in vindictive conflagration, but he had felt the bushranger's pain and cheered his desperate call. In the assurance of commitment, sunset's fire-toned palette infused him with a warmth at odds with the plummeting mercury. His deepening silhouette could easily have been that of a true bushranger, gazing wearily at the dying of the day and wondering if this sunset would be his last.

The report of a missing sedan hardly captured the attention of the Bathurst constabulary, let alone the broader population. The delayed report and the unreliable account provided by its owner hardly encouraged police to drop everything and give chase. They did, however, follow due process and alert all cars of a potentially stolen silver Toyota Camry. By this time, it had likely passed many Highway Patrol officers, with none having noticed the numberplate. Even if they noticed it now, of course, they'd be thrown a red herring. Until suspicions emerged, or fresher information came to hand, the missing car was unlikely to rouse interest.

The victim was less relaxed about the situation. After a consolatory bender, he got on the phone to his insurer, hanging up as soon as he heard their bad news. He called the police again and harangued them for their ineptitude. He contacted his mates and told them to 'bash any cunt ya see drivin' me wheels'. Then he went to the pub.

In a distant tract of mud and metal, the discarded tags of ill-gotten goods rested against a corroding, numberless, chassis. Destined to lay here a good while longer, if past interactions were anything to go by. Unknown pieces of a puzzle of future construction.

Far away in the distance, bright lights shone, and the cold mechanisms of modern commerce propelled the colonial outpost of Australia further and further away from its tangled roots.

There was a soft down of frost on Luke's swag when the sun re-emerged. The crisp morning air prickled like nettles on freshly washed skin. The chill was invigorating, a charge of energy and a swig of pure adrenalin to an empty stomach. He ate sparingly and packed swiftly, a spring in his step. A hymn of rebellion was on his lips, presumptive and self-aggrandising, yet passionate in equal measure. It followed him down the path to the leaf-strewn grotto to his car. His focus was sharp and spirits high. There was a procedural harmony to his movements, as though every step was preordained, moving in order, like planets on the thread of a solar chain. Remaining clear and focused would help him to avoid careless errors. A lack of attention to detail was a red rag to the bullish charges of justice. Rustic toreador of the Australian fringe, he'd deny them a physical target at which to rage.

Dust scattered and grey clouds hung heavy in the sky as the Camry's engine whirred and hummed into gear. Eucalypts arched their limbs at the thought of rain, filling the air with their scent, inebriate on remembered draughts. Tired and broken earth yearned for succour and quickly forgave false hope from the past. It was a land of the elements, in thrall to their ebb and at the call of their flow, dazzled by fire, swamped by flood, battered by winds and baked by the sun. This land had observed the past, prone and patient, vulnerable yet omnipotent. And it saw the future, because it knew how much and how little things change. When a timeline is forever, there are few events worth marking.

As his rear-view mirror framed the green mass left behind, he drove through the winter drear with clear intent. Momentum was unencumbered as he carefully tracked the speed limit. The countryside darkened, ominous and expectant, as he snaked a path with a surgeon's finesse. Road signs flashed past and fields of sheep and cattle languidly chewed through the day, oblivious to all storms impending. Less languid were the busted-up carcasses of roadkill, eaten from within and by scavengers torn. Mankind's advances had done no favours for the native fauna or flora; stagecoaches and steeds were less inclined to trample than SUVs and semitrailers.

Late-morning, he pulled into the township of Koorawatha. The ramshackle buildings and deserted streets spoke volumes about the decline of the central west. The few stately reminders of riches spent and memories lost only heightened the sense of decay. He ambled into the local pub and ordered a schooner. He watched the flow of beer to glass and wished he cared more for the contents than he did. Life until now had mostly been a journey of temperance, but the lure of a country boozer was too much to resist. The bartender, thankful for the company of someone other than the local drunks, made small talk, which was dutifully observed. Horse races beamed from television screens and an old wino in the corner looked up from his form guide.

'Number 5 is a dead cert for the next in Ballarat. You can take me word.'

'Sure, sure, Reg. How's that lucky streak of yours coming along, anyway?'

'It's about to turn, son. It's about to turn.'

Doors barely open for the day had already seen their share.

Luke stared at his half-empty glass, bade the publican farewell and left to the sound of another ripped up betting token.

Back in the car he travelled on, buzzing slightly from his frothy tipple and with eyelids quietly drooping. Once out of town, he pulled safely to the side of a barrel-straight road, reclined the front seat and relaxed, yawning his way into a brief and complete nap. The troubles of the world were immaterial, particles of sand adrift on vast waterways of time. In half-awake awareness he dwelt on the insignificance of life, the futility of existence, the bitter wheel of destiny. And those thoughts clung limpet-like to his mind, impossible to shake and voracious in their hunger. They confirmed his course with a rapturous force that shook him awake and upright at the wheel. Better to make a small splash in a large pond than to sink and drown in the ocean.

It was about a hundred metres from the turnoff and he decided that was as good a place as any to leave his car. There was a thick expanse of trees behind which it could be discreetly secured. The skies remained leaden, but the threat of rain had so far been empty. He parked, stepped out of the car and walked to the boot. There he fiddled and fossicked for a minute or two before emerging, stony-faced and resolute. He clad himself in dark jeans and a heavy, bulging coat of clay-tone hue. He wore a wide-brim hat of slow-burnt umber, almost matching the leather of his riding boots. His pace was measured as he strode along the side of the road, away from the car and its place of hiding. He felt exposed, and the suddenness and potency of these feelings came as something of a shock. He'd planned so meticulously and considered all possibilities, yet he'd never considered his emotions. Never considered that he might feel nervous, scared, uncertain or alone. Or if he had considered them, they'd been promptly disregarded. It was a touching moment of poignancy and a reminder that he would have more than the elements and constabulary to spar with. Despite this, he remained confident he could take on all comers. Doubt held no fear to his tumid consciousness.

He reached the turn and took the adjoining road, all compacted gravel and cats-eyes glaring. The edge of the surface was narrow and overgrown, providing minimal room for a surbated wayfarer, or even a skulking interloper gone rogue from a stolen car. Soon enough, widening space gave him an area from which to work, carved like the shadowed half of a two-up ring. He drummed up his most forlorn expression and stood like a hangdog statue of bushmen gone.

He unfurled an arm in time-honoured salute. And waited. The car didn't slow. If anything, it increased its speed as it neared. And then it was a tapering flash in the distance. He stared long after it was gone, before regaining composure. Minutes later, another vehicle loomed. And this one too barely paused to exhale, mocking him in a cloud of noxious fumes. A similar tale was told next time around, laced with an added dose of vitriol from a wound-down window. And the same from the other side of the divide. Short of building a roadblock or planting spikes, this was destined to be more ordeal than euphoric entrance into the hall of kings. Old Darkie Gardiner never knew he had it so good.

When a man stands and waits at the side of a road, before too long he thinks of himself as something less than a man. He becomes an option, a choice, a plaything of passers-by. He loses his power and the right to rule. It humbles him and, while making him desperate, it also sharpens his emotions to a fine and glistening point. As Luke lay down to rest that night, none removed from his previous station, his recently found vulnerability shone like a campfire in the scrub. And when he woke the next morning, the fizzing embers still warmed his ragged spirit. It humanised him and it also inspired him, as a reminder he was not the cornerstone of the universe. It didn't dissuade him from his chosen path, however it drove home the challenges and the skills he would need to succeed. Did he need to aim higher, to take things into his own hands? The greater the risk, the greater the reward. Or was it foolish to strike too hard, too soon? When common sense broke through the clouds, he realised that his heroes were men and less than men, they were slaves to emotion, to whim and to weather. They failed. Not just in their final conquest but at a multitude of inglorious, unchronicled steps along the way. To fail and struggle was to be in their image. He was closer to them than he previously thought.

A grumbling engine signalled another opportunity. Overnight rains had dampened his belongings, but not his spirit. Composed and consistent, he stood like a sodden scarecrow looking away from its field. The machine drew nearer, a ute of recent vintage and decent condition. Expecting the spit of scorn from its exhaust pipes, he involuntarily took a half-step back, almost coming unstuck in a shallow ditch. Perhaps it was a rush of sympathy, or perhaps it was preordained, but the wheels slowed. The driver pulled to the side of the road. And the passenger door flung open like a midnight lady's vice.

'Where you off to, mate?'

'Just into town if you'd be so kind.'

'Of course, heading that way myself. Jump in.'

'Thanks. On second thoughts...' he deviated, once in the passenger seat, hands swiftly beneath jacket and resurfacing with the caress of steel, 'Stand and deliver!'

He was less sure of himself than he sounded and hoped it wouldn't show. Fortunately, loaded pistols convey confidence that even quaking hands can't shake.

'Strewth. Settle down, mate.'

'I am settled. Now, do as I say and you won't get hurt.'

'Sure, sure. What do you want?'

'Well, I'm not here for a picnic. Give me your wallet.'

The driver shifted in the seat and reached for his back pocket.

'Here you go. Won't find much cash in there but.'

There was truth in those words. A $20 note was the sum of his providence. That and a royal flush of credit cards. One hand freed of its pistol, he pocketed the loot.

'Bloody useless. I'll take these, but seriously, use something other than hideous plastic.'

And in the spirit of his idols, he felt the call of faux gallantry.

'You can have the wallet back for being a good sport. I know you'll tell the cops and I don't blame you for that but know this: I'll be long gone before they can catch me.'

'Sure. I don't doubt it, mate. Now, can I go?'

With that, the assailant took a step back, guns still cocked, closed the door and retreated quickly to avoid the tyres of a rapidly accelerating vehicle. 'Stand and deliver,' he thought, 'what a stupid thing to say to a man in a car.'

As a ransacked bag of gold sinks with the weight of its burden, so too do another man's credit cards make for a less than seamless heist. Luke knew these had a limited half-life and that if they were to bear financial fruit, he'd need to rustle the tree without delay. He hurried back to the car, removed his hat, changed his coat and eased back onto the road. Careful not to take the same route as his victim, he headed west, as so many seekers of fortune had done before. His heart was pumping and his mind racing, charged by the thrill of success and blurred by the fog of changing times. It wasn't much of a success, but it was a starting point, a toe in the water. It had instilled a taste in the back of his throat that hankered and screamed for more.

Without PIN codes and with online ordering hardly an option (mailing address? What mailing address?), he figured his best bet was to stock up on supplies before lines of credit were cut. In the nearest town he found the nearest supermarket and purchased flour, meat, dried fruit and tea. He replenished his meagre toiletries and bought several bottles of still water. Plastic tapped and a cursory nod given to the attendant. He was safely on his way. He sidled into the closest hotel and ordered two schooners of ale, placing a few bets on reverse-legged nags, and one on a surging champion. Winnings were small, but they were money in the palm of his hand. Aware that this well would soon run barren, dregs were drained, glasses returned to a nonplussed bartender, and a beeline made for the exit. Through the pub's grimy portal, his image could be seen steering a silver bullet into the afternoon.

A kilometre or two out of town, at a designated area of rest, he spread the remains of the cards between two bins the colour of rusted blood. Cars passed during this process, but there was no call to halt or alarm. These heads would never turn for something so trivial. Having exhausted the afterglow of amber and the overthrow of restraint, thoughts turned to his next move. It was never in doubt. Remote enough yet not too far removed from town, he repeated the morning's ritual. This time, magic came to pass in the relative blink of an eye, with a middle-aged man kind enough to heed the hitcher's plea. There was no standing or delivering this time: 'Your money or your life' rang true to both modern methods and ancient sensitivities. Confronted with such an ultimatum and twin hollowed cylinders of unending blackness, the driver heeled the accelerator with such force that he was nearly clawing the core of the earth. Half-in, half-out, Luke rode the vehicle's manic swerve, managing to secure himself inside the car and regain control.

'Stop the car! Pull over now!'

The only response was flint-eyed determination.

'I mean it, stop or I swear I'll blow your brains out.'

'Never!'

The car hurtled down the road, straddling dividing lines in almost paroxysmal convulsions. Realising the situation was spiralling out of control and that oncoming traffic would either witness the unfolding drama or career headlong into it, he switched the grip on one of his pistols and brought it down like a hammer on the man's half naked scalp. Like a sack of russet spuds, he slunk to the wheel which Luke gripped while replacing the victim's feet with his own at the pedals. It was a close call, as a caravan-leading family approached from the other direction. Keeping a steady pace, he exuded false calm and forged a straight course back to gentle waters. He even gave a restive smile as they passed, unsure if it was expected or not. A doe-eyed infant stared in reply.

Parked at the side of the road, motor deadened but its owner still alive, Luke realised time was of the essence. He was a long way from his own transport and had unconscious company who would soon come roaring out of their slumber. He scoured the car for skeins or ties but came up empty. There went his first idea. Pockets were searched and delivered ten times the quarry of the previous target. With a surge of strength and desperation, he hefted the helpless body and rested it, supine, to wake in weeds at a future time. It was a longer than expected drive in a second stolen car to a point near where he had first seen it. There, he alighted, walked the remainder of the journey to the old silver Camry and, like a crab from its carapace, unburdened this faithful vessel of its living host. All earthly belongings slung over his shoulder and with a holster at his belt, he did not look back. At the end of the day, this was how he'd always wanted things to be.

- CHAPTER 4 -

'So, let me get this straight: this bloke reckons someone stopped his car, jumped in the passenger door armed with two shooters and demanded his money?'

'Yep, that's about the size of it.'

'Bloody hell. And he gave him what exactly?'

'Gave him his wallet, though apart from a bunch of cards, he only had twenty bucks.'

'Sign of the times, eh?'

'Yep. Probably for the best as well. The thief took the cards and used them, but only for minor purchases in Canowindra. They've now been stopped.'

'If it was me, I would've driven off.'

'I think he wishes he did the same. Then again, probably a smart fella not to.'

'No doubt. Did he recognise his assailant?'

'Nup, never seen him before. Was dressed up like a fancy style of bushman and didn't look like a local. Reckons he'd pick him if he saw him again.'

'What about him made him look like a visitor?'

'Not dirty enough, and too uniform. Don't know about you, but I don't see many blokes out here with clothes that match. Apparently, this bloke looked like he bought all his gear from a designer store.'

'And hasn't worn it much?'

'Would appear that way. Or keeps it very clean. We'll make enquiries of retailers to see if anyone has bought a bunch of outdoor wear recently.'

'Thanks, that would be good. So, what would make a bloke do something like that out here? It's a lot of risk for little reward, isn't it?'

'That's what the rest of us were thinking. Maybe he got the wrong target?'

'Or maybe he was just desperate. Were there any witnesses?'

'None. It's a quiet stretch of road, but that's still surprising.'

'Sounds like our man got kinda lucky. Well, both of them did, actually.'

'I guess all we can do is to put a call out for any reports of a well-dressed bushman who might be roaming the area. Obviously, the bank will cry out if he uses those cards. Any further description of how he looked?'

'Yeah, our man got a pretty good view actually. Doesn't seem his assailant was trying too hard to operate incognito. Height about 5' 10', medium build, but hard to say 'cos he was wearing a heavy coat. Caucasian, male obviously, dark brown hair and light beard, strong features. Mid to late twenties at a guess. Seemed well spoken, from the demands he made at least.'

'Well, that gives us a bit to go on, though out here it would make our lives a hell of a lot easier if he was some kind of foreigner. That description could fit any number of males in these parts.'

'That's true. Still, it's a strange crime, isn't it? Seems very bloody random.'

'It does. Keep an ear out for anything else though. It's pretty haphazard and he's hardly gained enough to retire on. A bloke that well-armed who's gone to a bit of trouble for not much gain is likely to up the ante before too long.'

'I'm with you there, boss.'

Senior Sergeant Owens pondered the incongruity of the crime about which he'd just heard. It was such a minor act in the scheme of things, but it carried a sinister whiff about it. It didn't seem to be the act of a young man getting his kicks. From the report he'd received, it seemed to be calculated—at least to the point of not being a complete spur of the moment attack. Why had the man robbed someone in a car? Surely it would be much more effective to do someone over in a dark alley if that was the intent? He obviously didn't want the car itself. He'd been given the wallet without a fight, so he surely could have increased demands if he'd wanted to. There was a mystery to this that tickled his policing senses. Without wishing for a violent escalation, he sat in intrigued puzzlement at how that mystery would unveil.

It didn't take long to find out more. A similar attack, a different response and a markedly different outcome. A victim in hospital, mildly concussed and deeply aggrieved.

'I know this might be hard, but can you describe what happened?'

'Yep. Pulled over to give this bloke a lift and next thing I know he's waving friggen guns in me face. Teach me for being a good Samaritan.'

'And do you remember what he looked like.'

'Yeah, looked like an extra from the Ned Kelly movie. And acted like he was in bloody Wolf Creek, like Ivan Milat or something.'

'What happened when he entered the car?'

'He pointed those things at me and told me he'd shoot if I didn't give him me money. 'Fuck that' I thought, 'I'm the one with the power here' and then I sped off, trying to shake him like.'

'You're a brave man. How did he react to that?'

'The way you'd expect. Didn't like it.'

'And then he hit you?'

'Yep. Next I remember I'm in a ditch at the side of the road and my head's hurting like hell.'

'And your car?'

'Gone like the Tassie tiger.'

'How did you get back to town then?'

'Well, when I come to, I waved down someone to give me a lift. Waved them down with my hands though – not a shotgun like that bloody lunatic.'

'Of course not. Thanks. I think that will do us for now. Get some rest and we might have some further questions later.'

'No worries. Just do me a favour and get me car back. Pretty helpless without one out here.'

The chestnut mare didn't quite seem sure what to make of her new surroundings. Gone was the complacency of a gently undulating paddock, scantily grassed in the rigours of a nascent drought. There had been regular bales of hay and a trough of tepid water constantly on hand. What they had lacked in luxury, her environs had made up for in reliability. She had learnt to recognise the spoken and unspoken commands of her owner and she'd learnt how to respond in the manner of a survivor born. From foaling to feeding, she was a paradigm of domestication. This may not have been the explicit design of her bloodline, but it had rapidly become second nature. It was an existence in which the struggle to survive had become a secondary concern, where life had become not a barrow to push but a carousel to ride. Even for a horse, cosseted and pampered–but still a horse, all the same–the rawness of life had been sucked from its bone.

With careful movements and warm reassurance, Luke had led her through the open gate and out of the enclosure. He whispered words as sweet as sugar and just as persuasive, with an appropriate level of firmness to hold her in his sway. The rope he'd secured was an arm's length too long, but he'd doubled it back and manufactured a knot that adequately served its purpose. In the yellow suffusion of dawn, snorts of steam cut through the fastness and plumed in the light. Calm as she was, the mare's sounds were secrets between she and her liberator. No ears but his heard her leave. And no eyes saw him close the gate and let the arms of the bush embrace two brown-hide beasts.

This world the horse now experienced was close, exhilarating and terrifying. Her new guardian and protector, while sympathetic to a fault, was a stranger. And when he attempted to saddle and mount, she bucked. Not expecting so much resistance, he pondered his failure from the floor of the sun-stained clearing, before whispering consolation and trying again. It was later in the morning by the time the process was through and he sat, as victor, bruised and tenderly triumphant. She rode well, understandably cautious at first, but in time became responsive to his touch and malleable to his bidding. The terrain was a challenge and negotiated with trepidation, though it was a sign of the roads they'd be needing to furrow. The easy paths had been blocked by fences or tarred in the name of progress. The meandering expanse of a squatter's fiefdom was now a grid of rules, laws and bylaws. It made for cleaner demarcation and fewer disputes. And it watered down the pioneer spirit that first settled this land. When a man has explored all corners, he sets his energies to fortifying their edges in protection of his gain.

They stepped down a rabble of jagged rocks, under skimming branches and over mouldering logs, stones skittering and kicking up dust. It was alien land to them, yet familiar, steeped as it was in century old blood and the thick paste of equine and masculine marrow. When he halted for refreshments and roped her to a gum, she nestled contentedly in the damp and grassy shadows. From his seat on a hollow log, his eyes took in the majesty of the rambling bush, while his mind spun circles of increasing circumference. This is what he had wanted. This was the vision he'd immersed himself in and the life he'd craved. The twinge in his muscles was a fruition of every promise. But he knew there'd be worse times from here. The hunger, the loneliness, the fear and desperation, the helplessness... These would come. And so too, perhaps, a sense of regret.

It was a fait accompli, in his mind at least, that he was by now a wanted man. Yet time travels more slowly than a man's great deeds. What he thought would be the talk of the town and an urgent call to arms was merely the subject of a routine police investigation. He predicted, correctly, that his recent exploits would be reported, but his sense of perspective was askew. While always self-centred, he'd withdrawn further within and walled up all paths of egress. He felt some remorse for the tapestry of crime he was sewing and while the violence of the second episode had been regrettable; it was also unavoidable. This was collateral damage from the shrapnel fire of a greater battle. The impact of his whims on the lives of the innocent was cause for scant concern.

Skirting the green edges of town, he moved surreptitiously through the rest of the day. Though the temptation raged, he wasn't yet ready to dive deep into the undergrowth. The bounty of civilisation had too much to deliver, and he'd barely breached the surface. In this brief excursion, he memorised routes and visualised hideouts, preparing for future glorious retreats. So much loomed uncertain, yet what could be controlled would be folly to leave undone.

By nightfall he was at camp and wrapped in pungent wafts of wood fire smoke. As he circled the fire in search of respite, so the plumes seemed to follow. They had a mind of their own, zoned in on their target and ceaseless in their pursuit. He'd reek of their touch long after the flames had been doused. Their bitter scent would be his perfume throughout the following day. And like the traps who would surely snap at his tail, when he thought he'd decamped they were back to surround him again.

Senior Sergeant Owens' phone rang once, twice, and on the third tone was answered.

'Well, we found the car. Or it was found for us.'

'You mean the one from the carjacking? That's pretty quick. Where was it found?'

'Yep, one and the same. Found not all that far from where we found its owner.'

'So, the bloke who stole it obviously didn't care to keep it?'

'To be fair, it was a dog-ugly colour. Wouldn't be seen dead in it myself.'

'Maybe not the most appropriate thing to say, mate. Its owner nearly *was* seen dead in it.'

'True. Sorry, Sarge. But it is strange that the fella who stole it didn't even try to hide it.'

'So, it was parked somewhere obvious?'

'Yeah, pretty much at the side of the road. It was actually a passer-by who noticed it and thought he recognised it. Knew the owner. Called the owner to check and yep, he was spot on the money.'

'If it was left there, the bloke who dumped it must have had other means of transportation. And he didn't care at all about covering his tracks. Do we have the car?'

'The bloke does. We have officers heading to his place now. Plan is to dust for prints and then search the area near where it was found.'

'Tell you what, let's you and me head out to that area to see what we can uncover. It might just be a ratbag kid, but with the guns and stuff there's something going on here that's not quite right.'

'Suits me. And if he was so careless with the car he was probably just as gung-ho leaving evidence, right?'

'Maybe, maybe not. But either way, I reckon there'll be a bit to see out there.'

A sense of anticipation rising within, Owens drove to the scene of the recent discovery. It was an unspectacular stretch of road, though its tree-lined edges and subtle twists and turns provided a semblance of cover. While there was intermittent traffic, there was not enough regularly to guarantee attention for a man parking a vehicle. For all intents and purposes, anything that happened here was likely to have been matter of fact and un-noteworthy. It struck Owens as a reasonable area to conduct a crime such as the one recently enacted. That said, for the life of him he still could not figure out the motive for such a reckless endeavour. Sure, as the old saying went: 'nothing ventured, nothing gained', but beyond a cheap thrill what could have been achieved? Men had expended much less effort for far, far greater gains.

The car itself had been removed, regrettably, by an owner desperate to be mobile again. The weight of its frame had indented the spongy earth, leaving telltale tyre marks like lines in the palm of a woodworker's hand. Having scoured the scene and failing to find detritus–a wrapper or cigarette butt would have been nice–the coppers broadened their search. If a man dumped a car at the side of a road he must have gone somewhere. Maybe he'd cried engine failure and hitched another ride? Possibly, but then how did he get here to start with? If he'd hitched to this location as well there'd be a lot of passengers' seats with his imprint on them. No, chances were that he had his own transport and had never intended to acquire another. The only problem was, after a solid two hours of searching, the area was as anonymous as before. Whether by fortune or design, this man seemed adept at covering his tracks.

Senior Sergeant Owens wasn't enthralled enough by the case to be disheartened by the dearth of evidence. He'd followed procedure, and, with the car having been located, it had restored an aura of normalcy. With the car being tested for prints, there were still avenues of identification to explore that were likely to yield results. He did, however, worry about what else the culprit had been up to, coupled with concern for what he might do next. Already, in two known crimes there were signs of escalation. Emboldened or embittered, this upward trajectory had plenty of scope to continue. While the deeds themselves didn't require specific consideration, there was a spinning propeller carving untold havoc within its arc. If he could kill the ignition quickly, he could put an end to the danger – and find out why it arose.

'G'day mate, what's your poison?'

In the cavernous guts of a weekday pub, this request sung out like a shrike. In reply, the newly arrived patron shuffled towards his inquisitor. He breathed sour and so close that it almost formed droplets on the bartender's stubble.

'Right, listen to me. I'm gonna come behind this bar and when I do, you're gonna do exactly as I say. Is that clear?'

'Ah, okay. Whatever you say.'

The bartender was no coward, but he was also a realist. While spoken softly, these demands carried an air of menace. He stood and glanced sidewards as his visitor encroached on sacred ground.

'Okay, while I watch, you will open the till and then leave your hands where I can see them, you got it?'

For emphasis, there was the sharp press of loaded steel.

A nod of the head was an adequate response.

'No funny business or you'll cop it. And that includes raising your voice, so don't even try.'

The register sprung open. Exposed and disappointing as a coffee-stained centrefold, its few notes pocketed, and its coins left cold.

'Right mate, you'll come with me. Make it look like we're doing business.'

'A bit fucken hard with that gun in my back.'

'It'll blow a hole in your arse if you're not careful. Now, move!'

And with that, he led away the publican into a room behind the bar. If he thought of resisting it didn't show. Minutes passed in an unmanned bar. The locals thought nothing of it. They thought nothing of anything, really. Except when they wanted a top up, but there was a hand on the taps before livers ached themselves sober.

'Just the usual, mate.'

'Sorry, I've just started–first shift today. The usual would be?'

'Carlton Draft. Schooner.'

'There you go mate. Don't worry about paying–it's on the house.'

'Bloody hell, Rosco won't be happy when he finds you're giving away free beer. Hey, check this out boys,' he said to his slovenly colleagues, 'we've got a new bartender handing out beers for free.'

'Plenty more where that came from. It's an open bar, gents.'

Somewhere between stunned disbelief and the most exciting news they'd heard in their life, a slow stream of pub-rats shuffled towards the bar.

'If you're shouting, make mine a Crownie.'

'Of course. Whatever takes your fancy. Rosco asked me to look after you as his loyal customers.'

In such a manner the afternoon wiled away. Amber liquid flowed, and it transformed the usually drowsy watering hole, into a smoky, rowdy, boisterous hive of activity. As word spread, numbers increased, though never to the point of bursting the seams. The good-natured barman plied his adherents with fuel to loosen even the tightest tongues. They rewarded him with tales tall and true, black and blue, old and new. The laughter was hearty and constant. In their revelry, no eyes turned to the doors as each was securely fastened. No one saw their provider's mood slightly stiffen and darken. Not a soul in that room had a care in the world that free liquor had not taken care of.

'Okay you lot. Party's over.'

All eyes turned to the figure atop the beer-soaked bar in dramatic ascension.

'I want you all in a line along that side of the room. Anyone who does otherwise will be shot. Do it!'

The shock of receiving free beer may have been greater, but this sudden breach of the peace shook even the most inebriated drinker.

'What the fuck?'

'You fair dinkum, mate?'

'Fair lark, cobber, but I'm not even sure I can stand.'

For all the quibbling, the responses were devoid of any real resistance.

'Move it!', and to the last of the dalliers, 'Do you want to be shot?'

'Who the fuck are you anyway? Come in here, give us free booze like some kinda Santa Claus for grown-ups, and then what? You gonna knock us off like clay pigeons now?'

'If you don't move now, I will shoot you where you sit.'

The assumed calmness in his voice came across as the coldness of a psychopath. It had the desired effect. The line was complete.

'Okay. I am going to walk down the line and I want each of you to empty your pockets into this beer jug. You try to jump me or do a runner and you get a bullet through you.'

One man piped up 'Hey, why did you give us free grog only to rob us after?'

'More fun this way. And it has been a fun afternoon, hasn't it, fellas?'

'I don't intend to hurt you', he continued, 'though I will if I have to. What you have been part of is the return of bushranging to this district. You have been in the court of Luke Barclay. Now, your loot or I'll shoot!'

As he paced down the line of beer-breathing wretches, some barely able to find their pockets to do his bidding, he collected a motley assortment of leather, paper, plastic and metal, clinking harshly in his glassy vestibule. His victims were compliant, or so he believed; and so he hoped, as it was too risky to frisk for secreted booty. He was on the alert for a breakout or rebellion, but none was forthcoming. He was aware of the possibility of intruders, even though he'd suspended a 'Closed' sign from the front door. Haste was imperative, and action must be decisive. Carrying his pitcher and walking backwards towards the exit, his gun remained fixed on those he'd just fleeced. He knew there was little time to lose. Battering the lock open, he barged into the street, regaining composure before bolting down a side street at a rate of knots.

Back inside the pub, a row of stunned mullets queued for someone to take the lead.

'What the fuck was that all about then?'

'The missus always told me I should drink less. Maybe she's right. Pubs aren't what they used to be.'

'Well, I'm gonna call the cops and see what can be done about this. We saw that bloke's face and spent a whole fucken arvo with him. Shouldn't be too hard to give a description and get 'im found.'

'Yeah, good call. That bludger got me pension money.'

'True. But it's usually Rosco who gets that anyway.'

'Hey, whatever happened to Rosco? In all the carry-on I forgot about that old bugger.'

They found him in the confines of his office, rope-bound and gagged. He was gratefully emancipated. His arms, chafed and stiff, were rotated briskly to encourage circulation. Wheezing lungs drew greedily on stagnant, abundant, air.

'Crikey,' he said, 'that bloke got us good.'

'Bloody oath. I do reckon he gave us more free beer than he stole though.'

'Yeah, not much of a crim.'

'Hey Rosco, any chance you can keep the free booze flowing?'

'Keep dreaming, mate. No bloody way.'

The police station was abuzz. Not since a former junior officer had disgraced himself at the last work Christmas party had there been so much spirited conjecture and gossip.

'So, are we sure it's the same bloke?'

'We need to follow routine procedure, but from the descriptions we've received, I'd say it's a safe bet.'

'Such a random series of crimes... did we get fingerprint results from the car robberies?'

'We did. Some rock-solid prints but they matched nothing we have on file. We have a team dusting the pub as we speak.'

'This bloke is something else. Beyond being a curiosity, I'm not sure how much of a threat he is, but I'd like him caught sooner rather than later.'

'Yes, boss. We have squad cars on the alert and with a full description. And the local hotels, in case he targets any more of them.'

'Did anyone see him get away? See what his mode of transport was?'

'No such luck I'm afraid. The old drunks only saw him barge out the door, and the street was practically deserted. No sign or sound of a car, though. We think he may have left on foot.'

'Which would mean he probably continued on foot or was parked away from the pub.'

'Yeah, I think that's probably right. We've scoured the area nearby and found nothing.'

'Widen the search. This bloke is now suspected of three crimes and is becoming a nuisance. Plus, he is armed and while he hasn't pulled the trigger yet, chances are he'll become more desperate as the walls close in.'

'Sure thing will do.'

'I'm guessing the press will be all over this–including the Sydney scum. We need to be seen to be on the front foot. I don't think we need a meet and greet just yet but direct any enquiries my way.'

'Better you talking to them than me.'

'I still don't understand what makes a man tie up a bartender, take over the bar, shout his customers for the afternoon and then rifle their wallets. Sounds like a bloke getting his kicks, but on a large scale. And you say no one in the pub recognised him?'

'Nup, never seen him before. They gave a name though: Luke Barclay. Told us he was proud to declare it, assuming it's not an assumed identity. You reckon he's from the area?'

'Could be. More than likely, actually. It's a big enough region. But we can check that. I'd say he's a disaffected young man, probably unemployed and with little of a home life, looking to get some thrills and test himself against the law. That can make for a dangerous individual–someone with nothing to lose. The more he gets away with the bolder he is likely to become. Again, I reckon we need to stop this little adventure quick smart.'

And with that, the Senior Sergeant returned to his growing pile of papers and expanding range of thoughts.

Sometime later in the day, word came in that the prints matched, linking villain number one with villain number two, yet still giving no hint to his whereabouts. Whoever he was, this Luke Barclay was either a new entrant to the seamier side of existence or as elusive as the Lithgow Panther. Chances were his cavalier attitude would bring him unstuck, sooner or later. The risk was that time intervening could redden his hands and make his existing body of work seem trivial by comparison. Owens was deeply aware of this. He knew also, if this was a kind of 'spree', the next episode would crave air like a claustrophobe on a coffin ship.

Assuming truth in the braggart's boast, records were scoured and unearthed a sole 'BARCLAY, Luke' in local and surrounding regions. As a lad of barely ten, he was likely cutting his teeth on computer games rather than violent crime. They made checks of his immediate kin, but they were clean as a sack full of whistles. Either the name was a ruse, or there was an interloper at work. Internet searches revealed several bearers of this freshly evocative moniker. Discreet enquiries were made, but unless this man had flown from England to commit minor crimes and returned at a speed preternatural, they uncovered nothing of weight. If this character was born and not formed, he kept a low online profile. And while logic would surely prevent a person brandishing their name in so brazen a fashion, it was a lead and needed to be exhausted. It wouldn't smoke out their man, but it would give a shape to the form they were hunting.

It was a junior officer who unearthed the nugget of intelligence that would provide a lead.

'Boss, I think I might have something.'

Owens steered his eyes from the computer screen to the bearer of news in front of him.

'I searched electoral rolls and found a Luke Barclay in Sydney. Twenty-four years old and seems to live with his parents in the suburb of Belfield.'

'Any other info? Occupation? Interests? I assume there's nothing prior that's slipped through the cracks?'

'Nup, no prior. Fella keeps a low profile with no social media presence. Here's the curious thing though—we got hold of his olds and they said he left home last Monday without saying where he was going.'

'Go on.'

'I asked if it was out of character and they said he goes away quite a lot, though this is the longest he's been gone.'

'Did they seem concerned?'

'Not really, though they don't seem the type to give much away – over the phone, at least.'

'I know the type. Did they have contact details for their son? A mobile phone number or anything?'

'Nothing. Said they kept bugging him to get a mobile, but he kept putting it off. I sensed a slight edge to his mother's voice when she said that.'

'Understandably. I'll sure as hell be making sure mine have phones when they're old enough. Though, truth be told, the only convincing will be for them to answer when their parents call.'

Owens took a moment to gather his thoughts before continuing.

'Did they have any thoughts on where he'd gone?'

'He liked to go bush, had all the best gear and everything, but beyond that they couldn't tell.'

'No idea where he'd been in the past?'

'Nup. He never told them. They weren't sure why, but over time they gave up asking. Figured he was old enough to know what he was doing.'

'Any employment that we can check on?'

'None that his parents know of. Was working at Bunnos but finished up there a few weeks ago.'

'Interesting. Any thoughts on his demeanour or what he was like as a kid?'

'They said he was friendly enough but had in recent years become a bit of a loner. No girlfriend they knew of, though they wouldn't discount it. He went away a lot. Obsessed with Aussie history and had his room decked out with bushranging paraphernalia.'

'Bushranging paraphernalia, eh?'

'Yep, Ned Kelly wanted posters, photocopied articles, replica artefacts – that sort of stuff.'

'Tim, you and me are gonna go for a drive to Sydney. There's just too much about this bloke that matches what we've got out here for it to be a coincidence.'

'Or someone has used his name and is pretending to be him?'

'Maybe. But, from my experience, the most obvious answer is usually the right one.'

- CHAPTER 5 -

Heart hammering like timpani in crescendo, bombastic and booming, he threw himself against a sap-glossed gum and slid to its base. His adrenal glands were charged to within an inch of breaking point. Nerve ends tingled and fizzed like a sparkler. Thought struggled to keep pace with momentum, with real time and action. And the placid mare, tethered and vacant, beholden to an unknowable past, gazed nonchalant at a ruckus at odds with her world. This pale emancipator was an enigma to her, as he was to many.

The chaos of realisation ran down his cheeks and swept through his system. He'd done it! He'd taken the next step and truly risen to the ranks of his prototypes. Elation, relief, and disbelief converged and bubbled in the cauldron of his mind. There had been a steady stream of doubts, but the underlying call to action had staunched them. He had visualised such things time and time again, and even if reality shone poor in comparison, it barely dimmed the lustre of triumph. Between deep insufflations of cool bush air there was a pure and boundless smile. This was a moment to savour and, he sensed, one of his last, as whatever deeds unfolded from here, the mark on his back would spread wider and wider, like an ink-stain on lily-white parchment.

He tallied the boon of his most recent heist. There was enough to replenish supplies, although making purchases would be fraught. He carried neither windfall nor wherewithal to drift into the sunset; at this rate his trade would be plied well beyond retirement age. Where thrill had reeled him in, gain held sway, insidious and ballooning all the time. He'd been savvy enough to expect this life to be all-encompassing, yet he was also naïve enough to be surprised by the outcome of his actions. This encounter with chaos was a shot to the system, a lease on life hitherto unknown. Although, when alone and at the mercy of his retrospective thoughts, every step was analysed, every move assessed, every corny phrase regretted. He couldn't so easily change his shape. He was no easy rider of the range. He was a sentient being of bone and skin, if deficient in concern for anyone else. While the risk at which he put others was having limited effect, the impact on him was the height of possession. A naturally introspective individual, by the candlelight of seclusion he stared ensorcelled into the musty illumination of his soul.

Realisation remained oblique. The view of what transpired at the pub was anything but a clear and consistent line. All seemed to happen in a flash, though he recalled his surprising sense of composure once in control of the bar. With time, even the possibility of his captive breaking free had slipped from his mind. While far from a born raconteur, he'd held court like a conqueror. A man of his own company, in that room and in that context, he had enjoyed the presence of others. And, oh yes, he'd bandied around his name, hadn't he? Put it out there to float on the ale-scented breeze. That had been part of the plan. His calling card bore no silent number. He wanted attention, and he teased for the chase. He was already shifty and on edge, expectant of hounds nipping at his tail. This momentary reflection could not last. It would curtail the euphoric idyll. He had to keep moving and to 'lead a merry dance', to coin an old bushranging phrase. With that came excitement and the construction of plans. He rose from his resting place, saddled the horse, bundled his belongings, and set off on a path due south, a song in his heart if not on his lips.

The house in Belfield wasn't much to look at. Nor were Mr and Mrs Barclay, if an unfair truth be told, though they came across as respectable citizens. They offered tea and sweet biscuits to the travel-worn investigators and ushered them into a living room dominated by plush upholstery and ornate china. They appeared stoic and sensible, not used to the company of the law and ready to bend over backwards to avoid the slightest sniff of trouble.

Senior Sergeant Owens dipped a Tim Tam in his cup and took a dripping bite.

'Thank you very much for your hospitality, Mr and Mrs Barclay. You shouldn't have.'

'Oh, well, you know, we don't get visitors very often. Especially important ones like you two. And, please: Len and Denise.'

'Of course. Thank you. Now, as you're aware, we just have a few questions about your son, Luke.'

'I hope he's not in any trouble or danger? The charming young man on the phone didn't really say.'

'Well, ma'am, he is a suspect in a couple of crimes out in the Central West.'

'Oh, dear. That doesn't sound like our boy.'

'What would sound like your boy, Mrs Barclay?'

'He's a good kid. His own man, that's for sure, but respectful and polite. Always kept his room tidy.'

'There were those guns though,' her husband interjected.

'Guns?'

'He has a few. Joined the local gun club and started getting into that a bit, as far as we know.'

'Do you know what sort of guns?'

'No, we'd be hard pressed to recognise one end from the other.'

'Mr and Mrs Barclay, would you mind if we have a look in your son's room? We'll have a few more questions to ask you, but it would be good to have a look at where Luke spent his time when at home.'

'No, not at all.'

With that, the accommodating, if increasingly concerned, couple rose from the couch and plodded down the hall to the cocoon from which their restless breed had emerged in full-grown form. They opened the door, revealing a dazzling mosaic of olden Australiana, a sensory overdose of items steeped in the harsh evolution of this land. As promised, there were wanted posters, faithfully replicated, along with reproduced photos, paintings, letters and newsprint. He had passed the more garish tokens of homage over in deference to the more primal, vital notations of history. It was a collection framed with a scholar's bent, rather than that of a modern-day 'fan'. Fact trumped facsimile, yet myth had been elevated above all. In these four walls, highwaymen were enthroned as kings. Their causes were noble, their victims hapless, their pursuers pathetic and their traitors blackened beyond recognition. It was an environment without objectivity, where beliefs went unchallenged and ran wild like blackberry vines. Taking in the oppressive volume of potent imagery, it was easy to see how the fruits of those vines could turn sour.

'Wow, what a collection.'

'No rock stars or Penthouse pets for this bloke,' ruminated the Senior Sergeant, under his breath. 'Has his room always been like this?'

'For a few years, yes, though he has added a lot.'

'And when he was at school?'

'I guess he didn't have the money to buy things, but there was an interest.'

'An interest in what, exactly?'

'Australia, I guess. And bushrangers, in particular.'

'My brother—his uncle—used to read him stories about that lot when he was a kid. Wild Colonial Boy and that kind of thing. He always went for Australiana—Man from Snowy River, Banjo Patterson, you know.'

'Any brothers or sisters?'

'No, just him. We always wanted another one or two, but Luke's an only child.'

'And a vivid imagination, I assume?'

'I think that's natural for a kid, isn't it? But yes, he was a dreamer. That's never really changed.'

'Does he have a car?'

'No, never really cared to get his licence. Always saw cars as more trouble than they're worth and I can't say I blame him.'

'So how did he travel when he went away?'

'Always by train, as far as I know—at least, from what little he told us.'

'Do you know where he went on these trips? Out of town I assume?'

'He never told us. We used to ask him – out of interest, not to give him a hard time or anything, but he always dodged the question. After a while and as he grew up, we came to the conclusion that unless we thought he was in trouble, it wasn't our place to ask. I hope that doesn't make is seem like bad parents.'

'No, not at all. Every situation, and every family, is different.'

'He has a swag that he takes, so we always assumed he goes camping. I believe that's what he's doing now, though I know you think differently.'

'Well, we're just making enquiries and your son's name has been mentioned. Can we see a photo or two of him?'

'Of course, come this way.'

With that, the procession moved back to the living room and to the mantelpiece where a roped-silver barrier framed a brooding image of blossoming adulthood.

'Sorry, he is a bit camera shy. This is the most recent photo we have. Must be five years old, from when he was about twenty-two. It's a shame we don't have more photos because he's such a handsome young man.'

'Does he look, more or less, like this now?'

'His hair's grown a bit longer and his beard is more defined, but our Luke hasn't changed too much.'

'I hate to do this, but do you mind if we borrow this for our investigation? We'll send it back once we've made a copy.'

'No, of course, go right ahead. We have copies of it already. Sometimes I feel they're all we have left to hold.'

'In what way?'

'Please don't think us bad parents—and please don't think ill of Luke either-but he doesn't really involve us in his life anymore.'

Owens raised his eyebrows, but also felt a connection grow within.

'Mine are younger than Luke, but I already know the feeling.'

'He is a good kid, a good man. I really hope he's not the person you're after.'

'So do we, but there are things we need to check out. At the very least, we'd like to find out where Luke is. The longer he's gone, the more we should worry about his safety.'

'Oh, I wouldn't worry too much about that. He has the blood of a bushman, that boy. It might be the middle of winter, but that boy will have the tools to survive.'

'Do you mind if we have another look at his room on the way out? Might take a photo or two as well if that's okay with you?'

'Go right ahead. It's been ever so nice to meet you both, even in such circumstances. Must be different living out in the country?'

'It's all I know, Mrs Barclay. It's all I know.'

Normal service had resumed at the hotel. Calls for the publican to take a day or two off (from his wife, not his clientele), had fallen on typically deaf ears. The daring escapade was the talk of a town more in shock than concern or fear. These were people more worried about immigration or encroaching technology than a blow-hard getting his kicks. They'd emerged unscathed, minus a few dollars here and there, and there was little chance of a repeat performance. It was a tale each would tell and embellish until the lid of their coffin slammed fatally shut. There was even a level of esteem for their attacker, for his decorum, and the guts he mustered to do what he did. In this age of gangs and drugs and two-bit thugs, the purity of such a crime was almost endearing. The whiteness of the perpetrator didn't hurt either.

The region's police had streamlined their attentions. They drew bows, long and misshapen, in attempts to flesh out a curriculum vitae of malfeasance. Every recent incident was assessed and considered for inclusion on this burgeoning rap sheet. Any theft, assault or bizarre depredation received either cursory glance or fine-tooth comb. Those displaying style over substance garnered special attention, owing to the possibility of a pattern taking shape. And if, perchance, a horse was reported stolen, they included this in the list of unsolved acts of lawlessness to be followed up with an eye more keenly attuned than normal.

Police stations of the golden west were busily comparing notes and ensuring no snippet of information slipped through the cracks. Which made it more surprising than usual that a silver Toyota Camry, found in a dense alcove at the side of a road, was reported and noted with minimal fanfare. Enquiries traced the licence plate to the owner of a semi-rural property notable only for its confluence of all types of metal. With more shrapnel than a World War I hospital, it was a haunting graveyard of skeletal remains, severed limbs and rusted body parts. Its groundskeeper was hard pressed to remember what was there, let alone what might have been missing.

'You telling me a numberplate of mine has been found? Seriously? Where was it found and how did it get there?'

'It was found on a car about 70 ks from here. We don't believe the car to be yours, but we're hoping you can fill in the gaps.'

'Really? This place isn't Fort Knox, as you can see, but I'm home most of the time and would hear the dogs if someone intruded. Bloody hell...,' he grumbled, shaking his head in disbelief.

'So, you know nothing about a silver Camry with these plates?'

'I know less than I know about quantum bloody physics.'

'Do you own a Toyota Camry, silver or otherwise?'

'No chance. Bloody Jap crap. Can't stand the things.'

'But these are your plates? They are registered in your name.'

'Buggered if I know, to be honest. Who remembers the numbers on those things, anyway?'

'Would you be able to check for us? According to the RTA these are yours and should be on a 1995 Holden Commodore.'

'Well, I have one of those. Let's have a Captain Cook.'

And with that the slightly more composed host led his guests through the rickety house, brushing hoarders' treasure as they went, until they were in open air and crossing a poorly grassed paddock. Treading carefully to avoid a litany of trip hazards, they weaved between numerous vehicles before arriving, close to the fence, at the tail of their quarry. It was a weather-buffeted and corroded paean to former working-class glory, the vessel drunkenly slavered over and rooted for year after year at a race track not far over the horizon. A symbol of manhood rising, or descendent masculine decline. And it bore no badges.

'Strewth.'

'I assume this had plates attached?'

'Unless I took them off, but I'm sure it's still registered. The plan was to do this baby up and get her back on the road.'

'This and all the other ones?', was the sarcastic reply. It went over the listener's head.

'No, just this one. The others are more for parts and stuff,'

'There's no chance you might have removed the plates and lent them to someone?'

'Lent them? Are you kidding? No chance in hell.'

'We're just covering all bases. If the car they're on is not yours and you didn't give the plates to someone, then we'll make enquiries to find out who might have stolen them.'

'Probably the bastard with the silver Camry!'

'Let's just wait and see. In the meantime, we'll need to keep these plates as evidence. Though, by the look of that car I doubt you'll be needing them anytime soon.'

A check of the car revealed an owner in suburban Bathurst, who through frothing lips and cascading vitriol was more than willing to outline his tale of woe. Yes, it was his car. No, he had no idea why other plates were on it and no, like a chef with dementia he had not a clue where his plates were now. The interior having been dusted for prints and numerous snapshots captured, they reconciled the silver bullet and its owner. And that was that. No lines were drawn, nor ne'er-do-well chains fused as one. The scope was wide enough, but intuition's gaze was narrow.

Lank and lissom rays caressed the bush canopy, and like newly hatched turtles on a march from the shore, only a fortunate few reached the expanse below. The air was a manuscript for the birdsong and calls, from the resonant chime of bell miners to the raucous laughing jackass and the subtle chirrup of smaller species heard but not seen. In the distance a winter stream bubbled, its urgent flow amplified by the stillness of the setting, the rocks beneath burnished by its pure velvet touch. Gum tree limbs jostled for position; arms outstretched to embrace the sun. Fanned out and verdant, ferns cast a ragged blanket over lower-flung regions, providing cover to prey and predator alike. This was a land of millennia, of dreaming and scheming, where death had its way, but life held sway. It had seen no empires come, let alone go. It dwelt within, having built itself beyond the clutches of progress. Where kindred had fallen, this land stood tall. It would still breach the sky while the trumps of archangels rumbled down from flame-lit heavens.

It had been quite an effort to lead the mare into this wilderness. It had been effort enough to evade suspicion on the perilous journey south, though the locals encountered had been civil and unemotive. With supplies relatively healthy, he asked nothing of them and continued to ford his way. He'd scooted around any built-up areas and had, where possible, chosen trails where a man on a horse might typically be found. As the journey wound on and his guard slowly slipped, he emerged onto minor roads, or rode closely beside them. Even in these brackish backwaters, he cast an incongruous figure and appeared as a throwback to unremembered times. Yet, life was such in these parts that nothing shocked the locals. They took the abnormal in stride and recounted it over a schooner of mirth during the evening's quenching. There were more important things in life than a stranger on a steed. If he travelled in such away, then so be it. If he could summon storms from barren clouds, these people would anoint him god. Anything else and he was a man like them, fragile and flawed. Best left in peace.

He stepped carefully over scattered stones and forest debris, leading his companion and watching each hoof find its place. What seemed a gentle incline proved anything but, its gradient slippery and studded with obstacles. Twigs and leaves cracked underfoot.

Unseen dwellers of the forest floor scurried away before titan doom crushed from above. The brush of fronds, both delicate and abrasive, swept like hands of regal adoration. And the timid beads of light flecked twin sets of hide as they edged further into this primordial amphitheatre.

Reaching a clearing that opened onto the creek, Luke halted and patted the horse fondly as she nuzzled against his warmth. His eyes locked with hers and then he pressed his face next to her cheek, whispering words of encouragement. If only she could respond in kind. Luke lost himself again in those sable eyes and sought connection with all who rode before. The stallions and colts who harnessed wind to aid their flight; the thoroughbreds with fading brands granted illicit liberation. Trotting cobs in docile service ploughing farms of which bushmen dreamed. This stately beast carried noble genes from which she would never be far removed. To be so close and to feel her pulse was to connect with times before them both. Luke couldn't help a momentary smile. This was a scene of which he'd dreamed. This was the Australia of old. To imagine Ben Hall in these mud-spattered boots would in no way be incongruous.

A gathering moil of guilt and uncertainty drew Luke out of his reverie. His mind began to fatten on less than pleasant thoughts. The sting of solitude was a slow-release venom entering his system and what had always held comfort was turning. He could feel it and the chill it bore, yet he also saw it as a passing zephyr of ill-born wind. To his way of thinking, he'd been alone all his life. A shark out of the ocean, he'd craved these lonely waters and the sustenance within. Yet, now that they lapped around him, their briny spume was more than he could drink and burnt his lips to taste. What he thought he'd known was in fact an illusion.

Staring deep into the billy can of life, solemn reflection gave way to solemn intention. Exhilaration of the recent heist had been as fleeting as it was fierce, a soaring toxin with a steep decline. There was no way back home. Those doors were locked, barred and barricaded. As needs must, sometimes we dare life to plot its course and act amazed when it takes the bait. When realisation strikes and cold dawn glimmers, we are left with no choice but to pick ourselves up and plough through the haze. This world was all Luke had wanted and all of which he'd dreamed. Lest it be forgotten, he chanted this mantra with insurgent passion, calling to wood nymphs for support. Then, having carved seven notches into tinder dry bark, he steeled his sturdy frame and led a compliant ally to the evening's camp.

Only a man can reason why he acts in certain ways. And only Luke knew why he withdrew so deep into the bush. Inexperienced in hardness of heart, flight took control over fight. What had been rigid calculation became a lure to respite. He could spin it as he liked and claim his mark had been made, but his plans had been grander and retreat more sudden than he'd imagined. Harboured now within the thick flanks of forest, he felt his fever dull and the throbbing quest for glory recede. The rage was fading. He felt its clotted gore thinning in his veins. And yet, without it, what did he have? He couldn't stay here. The fruits of the bush could sustain spirit for some time and flesh for longer, but they'd spoil and then, overripe, choke him like poison. This place was a mirror where nothing was seen. In hours of sight, however, it was a gorgon to stare at and turn him to stone.

Tired and worn down by hunger, Luke found strength enough to catch a fish in the creek. He cleaned it, gutted it and mummified it for a foil-bound journey into flames, like a piscine Kelly Gang at Ann Jones' Inn. The sweet fragrance of whitened flesh leapt to his nostrils as he unwrapped it, and buttery flakes gave way at the softest touch. He tore chunks of bread from a nearly stale loaf and scooped the meat up to his mouth, chewing intently and wishing for more. Head down and pensive, he glanced askew to watch the mare devour her miserable fare. He wondered if she longed for the sure confines of her paddock, the routine feed and the grooming brush. He wondered if she felt a bond with her captor, transferred over fence-wires to rough and virgin ground. And he wondered if she, who he had stolen, knew that she was all he cared for in this world.

The next day they followed the water's course and wound their way out of hermitage.

- CHAPTER 6 -

Senior Sergeant Owens sat alert at his desk, flicking through a growing pile of papers and sorting them by date. He was piecing together a tangible chain of events leading from young Barclay's departure from home to his arrival on the police radar. There was the minor question of guilt. There'd been no attempt at subterfuge in the pursuit of these crimes and a reckless disregard for the risk of identification. What lacked certainty was the extent he had planned this spree, along with the likely nature and location of the next chapter. Had he been a gambling man, Owens would have staked his house on there being another outrage, yet predicting its nature was akin to fluking a flush hand in a crooked poker den.

He skimmed again through the statement given by the young man's parents. Their disarming openness and old school naivete were affecting and almost off-putting. How could the fruit of such austere branches fall so corrupted? Not that the core of this soul was tar-black and astringent. It seemed a case of a good egg gone bad, rather than a bad egg gone noxious. Imagination bled, with no tourniquet to staunch it. Yet surely a moral compass would always right a southerly kink back to true north? Was that just him speaking from his own ethical pulpit? If it were his own kids—perhaps his eldest, all brawn and bravado—would he be close enough to smell arsenic on his breath? He didn't even know what they were doing half the time. Could his own lassitude foment similar unrest or shifting of purpose? There was little doubt this kid was unusual, but perhaps the path he'd taken was a more poetic excursion than one of his own would amble down? Owens–the father, not the cop–made a mental note to ask more, to engage more and, if need be, to pry more.

A knock at the door disrupted the sergeant's internal ruminations.

'Yeah?'

'Boss, we checked the prints.'

'And?'

'They match perfectly. And there were a lot to choose from. It's like he wanted to be caught.'

'Not that we've got him yet.'

'No, but he's not exactly trying to stay undetected, is he?'

'That he's not. It's hard to know exactly what he's playing at, to be honest, which makes this all the more intriguing.'

'You think he's playing some kind of game with us?'

'I don't know. Personally, I think he's getting some perverse thrill out of this, but he's definitely no career crim. I doubt he's even a particularly nasty bugger.'

'That more or less lines up with what witnesses have said.'

'Yeah, and his folks, though a parent doesn't always know a kid's true nature.'

'Tell me about it. So, where to from here?'

'Well, we have all we need for an arrest. Witnesses, prints, and I believe CCTV footage from the pub holdup as well.'

'Plus, hair samples in the car, for what that's worth.'

'Yeah, it all adds up. A warrant is being prepared as we speak. But it's almost like he hasn't cared about that stuff. Because he hasn't considered it–which I doubt, as from meeting his parents he seems to be quite a thorough planner–or because detection isn't his concern.'

'You think he almost has a death wish? That he wants to have his fun–and fuck the consequences?'

'That's what worries me. He could even be some kind of marginalised zealot with a bone to pick with society.'

'Sounds like the city type.'

'We get our share out here. But that's what I think makes him dangerous. I doubt he's looking for a way out and a quiet life in the hills breeding goats. For whatever reason, he may have bought a one-way ticket on a train running off the tracks.'

'But if he gave himself up now, he'd barely get a slap on the wrist, would he? He's hardly done a thing. He could say he's had his fun and regrets any trouble caused.'

'You're right, and I hope that's the case. I just don't want us dealing with a savage cornered beast.'

'Any thoughts on how we proceed from here?'

'We wait. We don't know where he went after the pub – unless you've heard reports?'

'Nothing yet, though we've asked the public for help.'

'All stations in the area have been sent his details. His parents said he's a skilled bushman, so there's every chance he's retreated to the bush for a bit.'

'So, he could be almost anywhere?'

'And probably freezing his tits off. Either way, chances are he's plotting his next trick.'

'You know what? He reminds me a bit of the old bushrangers, this bloke.'

'Yep, I think that's the idea. The greatest bunch of scumbags and losers who ever tainted this soil. Why a man would want to be one of them I'll never know.'

- CHAPTER 7 -

Deep in their plangent graves, either close to bone or in fossilised remembrance, the wretched remnants of eulogised souls stirred in bloated form. The years had passed with relative kindness. For all the crops sown, roadways paved, trees removed, engines primed, sprawling hordes and viscous webs, they'd kept their sheen and gained fresh glow. Through tempest and drought, snow and conflagration, they'd weathered the wrath of time with the self-same smirk they'd borne to their doom. Their skirmishes had been trite in the grand scheme of history, yet age had not wearied. Despite their lack of numbers, they'd feasted at will on the public's attention, while the rations of heroes far-flung and broken were meagre and shared like tins of bully beef. In the lazy, hazy mists of time they could not pick the faces of soldiers, their names a roll call unending. It was only with a target in sight and surrounding noise deadened that their shapes and shades could emerge to colour and contort. Their scope reduced; the scoundrels of the past had no such trouble. In a tussle for limited consciousness, those who truly exemplified courage and mateship rarely had a look in.

Chains latched and taut from the steadfast wooden roof, a silhouetted twin-head hippogriff steadied its haunches, reared, and charged with Herculean might. The chains held fast, but the wood did not. It ratcheted free of age-worn hinges in a tumult of erupting rubble. It trailed the decelerating beast, rattling like a rhythm section, before coming to a halt some distance from a freshly gaping maw. As one head lowered, the other detached and on limbs unfurled, paced to the scene of upheaval. Then, on bended knee and by the light of a silvery moon, this dusky searcher peered deep into a clammy and forbidden capsule. The blackness was suffocating. Torch beams peered deeper and drilled into obfuscated corners—and still the dark gave up no light.

In the distance a dog barked and sent a reminder. This was suburban terrain and hardly a safe place for fossicking. Edging away from the hole, there was no attempt to fill the breach or return the displaced plank to its charnel home. Instead, with increasing haste, the hippogriff reformed, raised its eyes and sped off into the night. Left behind was a scene of devastation over which stoic grey stone impassively stared. When the alchemy of dawn transmuted this land, it would give up no gold—just a ditch and ravaged coffin.

The press room emptied more quickly than it had filled, journalists dispersing to file breaking news and police officers filing out to break open a case with more twists and turns than Bells Line of Road. The tone of the fourth estate's enquiry had, overall, been almost jocular. Except for the usual underhand jabs that they refused to resist. There was a prevailing sense that this was a series of base-level pranks and that the perpetrator would soon come unstuck. The police had provided the identity and image of the alleged assailant, while disclosing that he was likely horse-borne and armed. In theory, that made detection a breeze, but then how had he eluded capture so long? And where in this vast, illusory land was he now? Equine conveyance and nightly abeyance would restrict habitat even without the hungry eyes of the law. The margins in which he skulked were narrowing to a verdant isthmus. Surely those confines would flush him out soon, when the pressure and lack of experience would force a false move.

It seemed more a matter of time than a matter of manpower snapping at his tail. And surely the press would go easy this time.

They didn't. *'Mysterious bushman terrorises the golden west', 'Police inadequacies laid bare by brazen bushman' and 'Stick 'em up! Bushranging returns to the Central West'* trumpeted front pages and online gazettes. Some mercy was given, but the tenor was one of no confidence in the region's law enforcement. Vested interests floated to the surface and bugbears itched and grated. There was intrigue in the spree's nature and theories of the motives behind it. In a wash of inflated house prices, guileless politicians, and boundless corporate greed, this served as a useful counterpoint, albeit with a sinister hue. It was both distraction and interaction with something more vital and real. Drama unfiltered, a nicotine rush to synapses both numbed and dependant.

It was a tense and sombre night in the Owens household, with rules of communication bowed to breaking point. Words balanced on tongues like an Olympic diver, tensed to somersault in liquid release. It took every inch of inner strength to force them back, to replace them with flippancies or loaded silence. Rules weren't meant to be broken, but this time there was public interest at stake, even if that line had been trotted out before and met with brusque resistance. In a world of grey there is comfort in black and white. To know where you stand without fear of contention is a warming nightcap on a wintry night. And for some that is enough: life's tapestry rolled tight and gathering dust out of sight. Keep the status quo and you'll never know what you're missing. In pinched, shallow runnels thus do many lives flow.

After their brood dispersed to do anything but sleep, the work-wearied couple retired to the couch. Weather slightly milder than usual, the fire was dormant. Stokers hung like ornaments on a smithy's Christmas tree. They had dimmed the lights to symbolise the fading of the day. And on worn brown leather seating, feet up on an antique coffee table, the valve could hold no longer.

'I wonder where that kid is and what he's up to.'

'This sounds like work talk.'

'It is, but it's relevant, don't you think? Everyone's talking about it.'

'It's work talk. We don't bring that in here. Call me at lunch tomorrow if you want.'

'But–'

'–I'm sorry, I know there's a bit on your mind, but you promised.'

'And I meant that promise, but surely we can relax it a bit? The kids are upstairs, and I think it's an important thing to talk about.'

'I'm sure you do, but if you draw a line in the sand, you can't just push it back when you want to. There's a young hoodlum out in the bush. Big deal. You're good at your job and you have good people with you–I'm sure you'll find him.'

'So am I. I dunno, I just thought it was a bit more interesting than most of my other cases – and a bit more relevant, with our kids at a really impressionable age.'

'I know they are, and I know you worry. So do I. And that's something we can always talk about as partners and as a family. But there needs to be separation from work and home, or one will take over the other. And there's no doubt which will win.'

'Yeah, I know. Sorry I brought it up.'

'It's okay.'

And with that, reading resumed, and communication ceased.

After five minutes, agitated and frustrated, Owens put down his book, rose from his seat and slunk out of the room. Moments later he returned, coat over his arm and car keys dangling from restless fingers.

'I'm going out for a while', he announced, leaving his words to loiter in the stuffy late-night atmosphere. He missed the blank expression and two mouthed syllables that ushered him out the door.

Motor purring and orchestral airs soaring, within minutes he knew the drive was doing him good. It washed away the strain of awkward conversation in tides of sonic mesmerism, as a focus on the road and the unique salve of solitude combined to realign his mind. As houses passed by and gave way to swooping darkness, poise returned and brought a smile to his face. He'd been wrong to raise work issues at home. He'd been a fool to think it a wise idea. It was a lapse in discipline and one he'd doubtless make again, even if he vowed not to. It reminded him of life's balance and the schism between how he earned a crust and who he fed it to. He wondered if this modern-day outlaw, this ignoble rogue with a penchant for unusual misdemeanours, had similar bonds with those close to him, or even awareness of how much they cared about him. That sweet and doting couple in the understated house with an understated (but carefully manicured) lawn and the intoxicating scent of roasting meat, like the promise of a tender embrace who'd done him no wrong and loved to a fault (if in mildly puzzling detachment). They may have lost him somewhere along the way and, to Owens' mind, they could have done more to keep the boy close, but he surely couldn't be so devoid of feeling as to leave them to suffer? Though its beat may be irregular, even the Devil has a heart.

Owens turned off the road at a lookout close to the mountains. He brought his car to a halt, silenced the engine, and sat in reflective quietude. To his right, beyond the plate of glass, a tenebrous expanse of chines, valleys and god-forsaken gullies extended beyond the daytime horizon. Alighting and pacing to a not so impenetrable barrier, his eyes tunnelled into the blackness. 'I know you're out there, somewhere', he whispered, in self-reassurance as much as any futile threat. Staring into this void, the scale of the operation was drilled home. If a man so chose, he could lie out here until charred by Armageddon. This man, however, showed no signs of being that type. He was an addict of action, a man on a mission and a slave to some crooked romantic vision. He'd resurface before too long. It was just a matter of predicting where and trapping him before he could retreat again. His rumoured predilection for hooved travel seemed to render him easy prey, yet he blazed a brazen path and still had not been traced. Like a sinner in search of hope, sometimes the things we think easiest are in fact the hardest to find.

Satiated by his own sweeping thoughts and nourished for the journey ahead, Owens snapped out of his reverie, left the nebulous murk behind and cut a headlit swathe back to the solace of home. There he found his wife asleep on the couch, a cat curled up in the crook of her arm and a novel face down on the table. In the dimly suffused light, she'd rarely looked more beautiful. This was where his heart beat. Somewhere above, in worlds of their own, yet trammelled to his, three blossoming souls strived for release from their helical cell. While they'd push and they'd pull until tethers were weakened, it should never be for want of love that they'd break away. Within these walls there was challenge enough; what lay beyond was, in some ways, of ephemeral consequence.

Owens cradled his wife's head, roused her gently and carried her half-woken form to bed. The warmth of their bodies infused him and left him groggy with contentment. Their hearts beat in unison, then their dreams drank of hope.

Next morning at the station, news was coming thick and fast. Discoveries had been made. The hounds had finally caught a distant scent. A team meeting was called, and information settled like birds on a wire. The Senior Sergeant conducted proceedings.

'So, I've been advised that we found evidence of hoof-prints after the grave desecration. Constable McKay?'

'That's right. From the cemetery the local cops looked at ways of egress. Given the lack of eyewitness reports in the town itself, they assumed the perpetrator didn't go east. Heading in a general southerly direction was possible, however crossing the Lachlan incognito would pose a problem. Similarly, following the Bogan Way was unlikely, so they took a punt that escape may have been made on the quieter roads to the north.'

'And?'

'They hit the jackpot. Well, sort of. They found a track.'

'A horse track I take it?'

'Yes. If that wasn't enough, horse shit to back it up.'

'When you've gotta go... Where did the track lead?'

'It dropped in and out, but it more or less headed north and then veered east at the School Road.'

'For those of us not familiar with Forbes, that is where exactly?'

'It pretty much skirts across the top of town. From there, he's headed north again, no doubt to avoid the Newell or find a safe place to cross.'

'Assuming he doesn't have any safe places to stay, you think he's headed east to find bushland?'

'Everything we know about this character so far suggests that he would seek shelter in the bush, so yes.'

'Do the tracks lead any further?'

'They don't, not in a consistent path at least. We do, however, have a possible sighting. A lady on the Back Yamma Road called in to report a man on a horse at around ten in the morning. She didn't approach him but says that he seemed to just be trotting along, minding his own business.'

'A decent description?'

'Heavy brown riding jacket, broad hat, dark trousers. Sounds like our man. And the horse she said was a beautiful light brown. They seemed comfortable together.'

'Are we aware of this bloke owning a horse? Last we heard he was stealing cars?'

'No, but one was used in the cemetery.'

'And his parents said he liked horse riding, even if he didn't have a nag of his own. Have we checked for any bought or stolen horses in the last couple of weeks?'

'We're working on it now.'

'Good. I want a report on that post haste. Now, where do we or the local cops think he was headed?'

'For cover, no doubt. After each job he seems to go to ground.'

'Right. And where around there might afford decent cover?'

'He was headed to the guts of Back Yamma Park, though I doubt it would be a long-term posting. Pretty much just a hangout for young hoods and cyclists.'

'Bit too modern for his type.'

'And not much cover. But further afield, there are two national parks that he could aim for: Nangar to the south and Goobang to the north.'

'I took the kids to Nangar when they were younger. I found it a decent retreat, but to them it was boring as all get out.'

'And at this time of year, in particular. Forbes police are scouring both parks and the Back Yamma place to see what they can find.'

'And what of the gravesite? Anything of note to come from there?'

'Not really. Apart from all the damage caused, but then he did nothing to hide that or clean it up.'

'Do we think he intended to cover his tracks?'

'Everything suggests they caught him in the act. Witnesses report seeing a man flee in haste, which suggests he was startled and motivated to get out fast.'

'And he's been careless with cleaning up in the past, not exactly hiding his crimes or his identity.'

'This bloke defies logic. I mean, he seems to be aping the old bushrangers, then he goes and rips open Ben Hall's grave.'

'Trying to get inspiration? Or right some perceived wrong?'

'Who knows? He's a fucken fruit loop, that's what. Might even be trying to throw us off the scent.'

'And all he's unleashed is more ink on his rap sheet.'

'Okay, team, let's get Forbes to keep us updated. I'm offering manpower to help in the hunt, so be prepared to get out and amongst it. McKay – chase up that search for stolen horses. And I'll head out west to see what else we can find. It's a wide operation now and we'll have to work closely with our neighbours, but he kicked things off here and this is our case, so I want us to nail this bastard.'

If the rumble of supportive murmurs could bring down gods, the heavens would just have fallen.

As Lady Godiva would attest, it's one thing to ride a horse through town and another to avoid detection. It's yet another to ride a horse through town with chains rattling like an asthmatic's windpipe. In the flurry of action and haste to depart, Luke couldn't detach the metal links. They fanned out behind as he rushed down the street, tentacled metallic horror in their clanging, scraping swarm. Once a safe distance from the scene, he'd dismounted and unhooked them from the stirrups, flinging this makeshift pulley into a weed-strewn culvert. The roar of adrenalin spiked again and powered him on to what he considered stiller waters. He was sure he'd been spotted throughout this flight, but the boldness of vigour left him blind to these concerns. He'd steadied his pulse, and with hat doffed to normalcy in a scene so far from it, the mounted figure trotted at ease through the grey-tone and weatherboard backblocks of town. As one who'd never fitted in before, it troubled him little to stand out now.

What local knowledge he had was largely framed by maps and guided by compass, embellished from time to time by what loomed in sight. Necessity played its part, shepherding him to havens away from inquisitive eyes. That these formed his preferred habitat was a pleasant bonus. That authorities would expect this and search for him there was, however, a growing concern. So it was that, after thinking of more nights under swag and pregnant firmament, he decided to change tack. So close to the bush as to drink its botanical breath, he dog-legged north like a bird returning from winter. He shadowed the green fringe and kept an eagle eye on his surroundings, more alert to those who couldn't see him than to those who might. He was a wedge-tail gliding the thermals and coiled up to plummet. Each farm pricked his senses with the hint of succour, but as doubt follows hope, thus hope precedes disappointment. The search went on.

Later that night, showered for the first time in weeks, well fed and resting saddle-sore haunches, Luke reclined within illicitly taken accommodation. It was a sprawling homestead with tenants nowhere to be seen, and he'd breached the lock with consummate ease. No smoke rose from the chimney, but the environs were warm. This was like a weekend away, a soul-reviver in a cutthroat existence, where the cares of the world faded until they swung with renewed malice in a wrecking ball curve. He sorted his belongings and washed reeking clothes. In mock domesticity he found an ointment for his wounds, soothing and softening his weather-beaten psyche. It took him back to the hours of his youth, when comfort was taken for granted and dreams were all gold. In this moment, he might have realised that humans have evolved from beast-hood and with this lineage clean and base nature intact, it remains impossible to truly escape the civilised world that has received us. Instead, he used his privilege to dwell on the past, on the sepia-stained images of a time that still felt within reach.

Luke sat at the window and peered into the dark whence he came. He had been convinced that liberating his hero would right the wrongs of the past, would open conversation and lead to belated redemption, but had it really been worth the effort? Cowardly betrayal and defenceless murder would echo the same no matter where the body lay, as would thievery and violence. Besides, did most people even care about a dead man's reputation? Then there was a question of risk and reward. Was he far enough away to avoid the fallout that would inevitably come? Did he even care? He was tempted to yell out of this portal to the world that he was here, ready and waiting for the worst they could deliver. He kept expecting a steel cylinder, a blaze of light or a call to submission breaching the night. Yet when exhaustion overcame his paranoia–blistered mind, he lay free under pastel flannel sheets.

With dawn came refreshed zeal, and the haughtiness expected of an outlaw at large. While ego craved a sign that he was talk of the town, no sign meant no reason to give up the game. Besides, for all he knew, his name was rolling off every tongue between here and the ocean. He flicked through television channels in search of recognition, only to cloy in the morass of a culture forged in foam. It disgusted him. He had no place here. He may have had no place in the past either, but it was sure as hell more poignant and purposeful, no matter which way you looked at it. He switched off hoping for a faithful portrayal on the cover of a dignified bulletin. That was probably the best to which he could aspire. Was any publicity good publicity? Even when clinging to society's underbelly, he was inclined to think not.

Pursuing a line of thought only recently sown, he rummaged through a corner desk before sitting down and letting inspiration flow. Many scrunched and shredded pages later, he sat back to admire a blazing manifesto.

To the public at large,

I am a man sorely wronged and representing those wronged before me. It is with a heavy heart and no lack of compassion that I have chosen this path. It is a path taken with the best of intentions, in the worst of times, to enlighten the masses to the ways of yore that should never have been displaced. I am a conduit for our ancestors and their struggle that birthed this nation. Through me, they are having their say again. You may think me a petty criminal. You may think me mentally deranged. You may think of me as laughingstock. Think what you like, because the truth will out regardless.

This is no crusade of guerrilla warfare. It is a quest for enlightenment in a world gone mad. Cast your gaze to the pure ways of old and away from false modernity. Times have changed, but the essence of life has not. Through my actions I am raising a flag for a better world, while righting the wrongs committed to men who dared to stand up to an unjust system. That crimes are involved, and people suffer is regrettable, but there are no innocent parties any more.

I bear no grudge with authority or the law, except that you represent the society I despise. You uphold its depravity, you foster false values, you undermine all that this great nation was built on. You may say you have no choice, but there is always a choice. It's our right as Australians, what our forefathers fought and died for – and it is what I have taken when following this path.

This story has merely begun. You may try to catch me, and I dare you to do your worst, but you need to know where to find me first. I am a will-o'-the-wisp of the Australian bush, like the yowie or Lithgow panther. This is my home. And I am better equipped to live here than you will ever be.

I make no demands and expect no mercy.
Respectfully, a son of this land
L.B.

Whatever misgivings had surfaced the night before still dwelt within but were drowned out by deafening tones of strident dedication. There could be no cracks in the surface, no signs of doubt or commitment wavering. This was his platform, towering and proud, from which to convey a message without filter, a mission statement from the heart. There were words and phrases he'd mulled over (will o' the wisp? Not exactly what he was after. Maybe mystery would have been better?) and he'd leant towards power over precision. Ink dried and crusting, he scrawled a second copy. Then he creased the paper and found an appropriate envelope. He was lucky his unwitting hosts had some old school persuasions. They also had postage stamps, and he fixed one to the top right corner of the envelope, before mulling over the most fitting recipient. As tempting as police or politicians might be, he knew where true power lay in this feckless age. The pen remained mightier than the sword.

Like tadpoles racing to disperse before the rush of predatory force, Luke knew that to tarry would be to play with fire. He was already fortunate to have found a vacancy at what he had christened 'The Highwayman's Hilton'. It had served its purpose. And unlike graceless visitors scattering to leave their host in the lurch, he cleaned and left everything just as he'd found it, apart from a pantry half as full as before and a window jamb scarred by his mode of entrance. As he quietly pulled the door closed behind him, there was a tinge of sadness and the gleam of vulnerability. It felt like he was starting again. Except that he wasn't, and by cumulation of misdemeanours he walked out a marked man. Faith in his ability was unharmed, but while devoid of physical evidence, he visualised the roughened walls of fate closing in. He'd taunted by right and thrown care to the wind–and it filled him with a power unbridled and fierce. He could curb those tendencies and slither in stealth, but would it really serve him well? Did he care more about a lengthy spree than a euphoric one? For answer, he looked at the men who'd set him on his way. And then, on sullen, stolen hooves, he rode out as bold as day.

- CHAPTER 8 -

Light rain sauntered down to heavy earth below, resting innocuous on a rural tableau. Crops screamed for more, barely satisfied even in the arms of deliverance. This brutal land bowed to only one queen; whose tyranny swelled like a soul in surfeit. Why would anyone set camp under such disparate whims? Why endure seasons on end with no fodder but hope? Hidden within was an acidic truth: choice was oft whispered but rarely caught, and those who endured had their own reasons why. The limits of choice held as much claim as pigheaded resistance. The *idea* of choice and *potential* to tap it are often more potent than the practicality of use. And so, year in, year out, spines crooked and palates dry, a hardy, mournful breed wrestled with choices and remained where they were. It made them by turns resilient and defeatist. With heads ever skywards, they strived to plant seeds by sight, expecting to fail but trying all the same. Until the idea overcame inertia, they'd brooch and obsess over it while suffering as one. Their right to choose was a pipedream, not a path. And the right to remain was a rod for buckling backs.

In this land of higher drama, a brigand on the loose was more curiosity than concern. Life held enough challenges as it was. The only emancipator sought was one who could release streams from above. While the quirks of bureaucracy irked from time to time, authority was protector, not oppressor. The churn of the city was as alien to these folks as their farms to an antique squatter. They were patriots to the quick and loyal to a fault. Opinions went unchecked in the dearth of dissent, and biases flourished because they could. It was a dour environment, flare-lit occasionally by raw human emotion that radiated like summer rays on a salt-bed lake. While methods and appearances may have evolved, the kernel of existence had barely changed.

If Luke had expected to ruffle these dusty feathers he was in for a rude awakening. If he'd expected to be borne aloft as a conquering hero, well, he'd find no shoulders here on which to stand. Being reluctant to engage with the public, he relied on a wellspring of support miraculously spurting from the ground. The truth was, if it didn't affect them directly, people just didn't have the energy to care.

Down towards the Lachlan he rode. At a deserted but well-grassed paddock, he dismounted, busted open the lock and led his ungulate ally like bloodstock at sale time. Unsaddled and stoic, she glistened in a veil of rain. She'd been proud and unyielding since day one, as honest and constant as time itself. She had met every expectation he had of her kind and had played true her role in this saga. She had been a perfect bushranger's accomplice, but if Luke was to hide from the law, he knew she could soon become a burden. He patted the horse's neck and drew close to her breath, tears trickling down his already damp cheek. 'Thank you', he whispered and hugged her again, before turning his back and striding away. When she followed, he stopped, raised the palm of his hand, and retreated again. In the end it was a mad rush to close the gate and leave before the tears returned. He did not—could not—look back.

Once again alone, weighed down by belongings and the need to survive, Luke trudged onward through coagulating soil.

Like a disoriented hiker on the hunt for a mountain trail, Luke scanned this way and that for only he knew what. Long reedy grass that tickled to the touch through his thick coat and trousers obscured his vision. Traffic was minimal and, no longer horse bound, he felt scant need to hide from view. He knew that to act as normal would diminish suspicion. The rain had increased, and droplets bounced off his hat to join puddles below. A sodden mess of razed sienna. His powder was dry, but little else.

After an hours' march, he realised the futility of continuing in this manner to destination only hazily known. Spying a farmhouse suitably tucked away, he crept with almost feline grace toward the building. Zeroing in on a new set of wheels, he drew nearer. The rain beat harder. It was perfect cover, yet it could do nothing to protect him from a sudden flood of light and the sound of tires sloshing through washpools at seemingly breakneck speed. He jolted with an involuntary start and quickly scrambled for shelter behind the carport wall. He was just in time. Heart pummelling his ribs, he gathered composure and reached inside his saturated coat. Gun in hand, he wondered if now was his time to use it. He heard the car pull up and its owner get out, through the paper-thin walls of the carport. Time stood to attention and footsteps dropped like bombs. It was impossible to tell if they were coming closer or leading away. It was only when a door in the distance opened and closed that Luke knew he was safe. Moments later, breathing again, his sweaty grip slid off the steel of his weapon. Nerves frazzled; this prize was too risky. There would be others with much less at stake.

The next house he went to was vacant and enticing. There was a four-wheel drive parked in the kidney-shaped stretch of gravel at the front. 'Don't you dare be a manual' he intoned with mantric fervour. His luck was in. Hotwired and ticking over, the car shook under his clumsy right foot before flattening a row of plants on its serpentine course to the roadway. Once there, Luke spun the wheel clockwise and spluttered into mechanical procession, checking the car's mirrors more often than the road ahead. Romance was gone. Cold reality had unpicked the seams. He'd done fair service to the days of old, but constraints of the modern age were tightening. Colonial oaths were still stoically sworn, but the test of their power and the depth of their potency would be to adapt and thrive in this loyalty-bereft time.

The excited reporter was two coffees into to his morning shift when he approached his colleague, letter in one hand, half-eaten muffin in the other.

'Mate, you will never guess what just landed on my desk.'

'No idea. A novelty dildo?'

'Ha, you wish. Remember that guy committing weird crimes out west?'

'Sure do. You gonna tell me they caught him rooting a goanna?'

'Not quite. Save that one for the Telegraph. No, believe it or not, that tyre-kicker sent us a letter.'

'You mean an email?'

'Nup, a real-life pen and paper letter.'

The bearer of the letter took a bite of his muffin.

'Really? I thought only people the other side of fifty still wrote those.'

'Me too, but this is not your garden-variety nutcase. Have a read of this.'

Silence took over as they scanned the page, raised eyebrows marking points of note, a hand brushing away stray crumbs as they fell.

'Interesting, eh?'

'His message is all over the place, but he writes pretty well.'

'He does. Off with the fairies and full of himself though he is.'

'He's not alone there.'

'Ha, you can say that again. What do you think he's after with all this?'

'I guess he just wants to have his say and be heard? I dunno. I mean, it's not a typical terrorist threat or ransom note. It's kind of cute really, in a hokey sort of way.'

'A cry for help you reckon?'

'I think it's probably some wannabe tough guy schtick. He thinks that by sending us this we'll publish it and he'll become some oddball celebrity.'

'Ready to appear on the next reality tv show or something? Survivor Condobolin.'

'Survivor Long Bay or Survivor Goulburn Supermax more like it.'

'So, what do we do? Publish it?'

'Thought you said we're not the Tele? We give it to the cops. But we take a copy first. I doubt there's much readership for this shit these days, but you never know–if he starts offing people that would quickly change.'

'Or rooting goannas.'

'Yep. Especially if he does that.'

Two hours later the self-same missive was delivered to the central police station, inky prints of journalists smudging each page. It was read with interest and a twist of mirth, before being scanned to colleagues in a division over the Range. By the time the letter reached the Senior Sergeant's desk it was better travelled than smallpox.

Owens read, re-read and further digested the words scrawled on the page in front of him. While there were no explicit demands, there was a malevolent undertone that did not sit well. Yes, the message played out as a scattergun cry to the world, but it carried a troubling lack of empathy, regardless of initial protestations. While there was nothing in Owens' knowledge of the young man's past to suggest he was 'sorely wronged', not that the man himself didn't believe this to be the case. Most likely, this was meant in a broader sense that tied in with the stated mission. Most disturbingly, the off-hand references to crime and what he might do sent a chill down the grizzled cop's spine. This was the talk of a man who, if cornered, would likely choose artillery over armistice. He had no need to spell out threats or verbalise demands. The Devil's tongue had moistened the envelope and flicked venom between each line.

With acres of wilderness flensed to the bone, dredged dry and discarded, the appearance of a letter was a welcome relief for the sergeant. It was a link to civilisation and a sign that, for a time at least, this spectre walked among them. He had come out from the bush, it would seem. Was he now holed up in a house and if so, what was the context? He'd taken hostages before, so perhaps he had again? For all the flaunting, taunting and patent disregard for the risk of recognition, this infuriating felon remained on the loose, with an untold capacity for further strife. That his letter was an ego stroke and cry from the hilltops. It was a call to give chase rather than final declaration. It gave hope, yet it also rose as an ominous pillar from which greater atrocities could emerge. All leads were being chased, including the source of stationery, the mailing point and theoretic termini of those deceiving tracks. By now a veritable swarm was spreading across the district. And if their ink-blot stain was unable to seep to far enough reaches, marauders from the east would crest blue sunrise across the hills and do the job themselves. Not on his watch, they wouldn't.

Swivelling in a chair that eclipsed him for service, Owens gazed out a dust-smeared windowpane and pondered the next move. They had found a horse. It was a long way from home. It looked contented and well-treated, but it was still a long way from home. And when traced, that home was found to be one which had reported a beast stolen around the time of this young tearaway's arrival. This news was no circuit-breaker, but it was interesting. Unless he'd discarded one steed for another–unlikely, as his recent mount was far from hobbled–Barclay now travelled by other means. The letter most likely meant a motor primed with curdled fuel. The game was not changed, but the pace now met the age.

Before anything else, the area needed to be combed for stolen cars. Knowing where the mare was found, they could scratch a circle around surrounding properties, with a slowly spreading circumference, detecting empty garages, carports, and divergent parking sites. Find the car and they'd be on their way to finding their man, bloodhounds on a caustic petrol scent. Shapes may shift, and scents may scatter, but apart from posting armed sentinels at various points, this was the crystalline approach to take. Owens gathered his thoughts, raised the handset, and whipped up a call to action.

- CHAPTER 9 -

Change, once the daunting is done, re-energises tired souls. What previously dragged, lagged and grated relinquishes to the onset of excitement; blood rushing, a kaleidoscope of wonderment and promise takes form. Bring the most jaded creature a vial of this altering elixir and trick them to taste, then watch new life run wild in their eyes. Yet for the rambler, change itself becomes a recurrent rhythm. As he travelled on, a web of confused emotions immersed Luke. Freedom, power, and acceleration all in one.

The modern-day bushranger had travelled far, while keeping within his sphere of operation. Hugging the lines of roads less travelled, he traversed the region and settled near the icy fastness of Oberon. It was after dark by the time he arrived, jittery and impatient for further activity. While he was successfully jaunting around the Central West, achievements had dwindled in recent time. His story had stagnated, and history books frown on even a minute of inaction. There was too much flicker and not enough flame. He realised that life reverts to form, and persistent inner anger must maintain that rage. This was a course he'd chosen and a commitment he'd made, but how much did he froth at the mouth and bubble with hate? Barely troubled on his journey so far, there'd been no incitement to vengeance or to crush those who stood in his way. In making life easy they'd removed its purpose. The fire would need to come from another source.

A short distance out of town, that fire rose to lick. It compelled his four limbs to motion and delivered him to a foreign door. Hunger pangs stabbed like blades, his provisions now beginning to wane. Yet there was more than an empty stomach at play. Tensed and intent, the heavy-coated outlaw pressed flat against an outer wall, ears like wheat fields harking to the soughing wind. He took a deep breath. And then another. On the third breath he spun around and charged headlong at the iron-hinged entrance, a berserker on high. One surge was not enough, but it drew a response from within: a startled scream that shattered the night. Before there was a chance to think, he battered again, using every sinew to crash the stubbornness of solid oak. In the space of split seconds, he felt resistance give way and a vacuum emerge in front of him. Time then slowed as dust subsided and the ringing in his ears faded out. Eyes catching up, he fixed them on materialising figures cruelly ripped from domestic contentment.

As unexpected as his arrival, the verbal greeting was unnervingly civil.

'Good evening. I'm sorry to intrude.'

Stunned, it took a moment for any of the three tenants to respond.

'What the...' was all they could muster. Their guest was more loquacious. He also had the benefit of two cocked pistols.

'It's okay, you'll be alright, but I'm a man with no home and quite a hunger to feed.'

'Yeah, and we now have a home with no door in the middle of winter, thanks to you,' piped up the eldest of three, and the only male.

'Sorry about that, but I guarantee I'll have it barred up before you sleep. For now, I could really use something to eat.'

'There's a pub down the road for that.'

'Nothing on the menu that grabs me.'

'How'd you know there'd be anything here you like? We don't have much.'

'Lucky guess, I suppose. But now I'm here, there's plenty to take my fancy,' replied the assailant, ogling the other occupants.

'Oi! You do whatever you want to me, but you touch either of my girls and I swear I will kill you.'

'Come on, please, I'm not that kind of man. Though, they might be that kind of young lady. Let's leave the choice with them, eh?'

The father seethed in response but said nothing.

'I really don't want to hurt you, but if you call the cops or raise the alarm you will all enjoy the taste of lead. Though, isolated as you are, I dare you to do your worst.'

The seething died down. Realisation sunk in.

'Now, I need something to eat, but I can't risk one of you deciding to play hero. I have some rope here and I am going to tie you up, one by one. Girls, think of it as an education.'

'You arsehole. Let the girls go. They've done you no harm.'

'I will, I promise, but think about it – what would you do in my situation?'

'I wouldn't break down a stranger's front door, for starters. And I sure as hell wouldn't threaten his kids.'

'Then you're a better man than me. Now, move!'

With that, he corralled the three hostages into the corner of the room. In the smallest of mercies, that corner was near a smouldering fireplace, though the heat it emitted was slim consolation. Emasculated, the father slunk to the ground and drew close to his frightened daughters. Instinct took over and survival was king. As the threat of aggression receded and piston-thud heart rates retreated, this became a chrysalis to mature from, not a pupate tomb. Violation, frustration and annoyance would remain for many long days, but for now they were prone to do more harm than good. Ties tested, held fast and once tried, closed in tighter; like rodents in a python's grip, the more they fought the more it trapped them. All they had left was to listen to rummaging and guess at what for, then hope beyond hope no foul depredations were in store. Some battles are worth waging with every skerrick of life. Others are mere scuffles that time will annul. The trick of existence is to tell which one is which.

It seemed like hours but was in fact less than ten minutes by the time he returned. Gorging on toast and with bulging bags swinging, the interloper strutted into the living room, within two spans of his captives. He casually took a seat and crunched again on buttery communion. Nearer entrance than fireplace and with no free hands to hold his jacket tight, he shivered perceptibly.

'I thank you for the hospitality. It really has done wonders.'

'To you, maybe. What about us? What about our door?'

'Yeah, you big coward,' chimed in one of the girls, voice flooding to her lips.

'It's alright, honey, let me handle this.'

She was undeterred, 'You think you're tough, but you're weak as piss. Tying up a man and his kids? Wow, what a legend.'

A wry smile came to the intruder's face. There was much to admire about this display of will, and the provocation, instead of riling him, fattened his ego. He found that flattery lay in the strangest of places and that to be feared and despised proffered perverse charms.

'Madam, I am shocked. I promise I meant no harm, but I am a father's son wronged and cannot be blamed for what I do.'

'You're a big fucking loser, more like it!'

That lit a fuse. No toast in his grasp anymore. An arm quickly stiffened and levelled.

'Old man, it would do you well to give your daughter's tongue a trim.'

'Wait! No! If you're going to shoot anyone, let it be me. I raised them. Blame me for the way she speaks to you.'

'Sure, but the thing is, we are all responsible for our own actions. I'll sure as hell find that out when the law deals with me. So, while you might be a hopeless wretch of a dad, that girl is old enough to know better.'

With that, a shot rang out.

Some distance down the road, nestled safely in town, Oberon police station was a picture of small-time austerity. Rarely stirred from soporific repose, traffic offences were excitement enough. Dreamers moved to the big smoke. For those who stayed behind, to live and work in their own community sufficed. And with the failure of government to foster growth beyond creaking city limits, it was on the shoulders of these few that the fate of inland villages was borne. Prosperity parched by auriferous plunder, they stumbled on in ever decreasing circles. They rose and fell with the health of the land, the passing of seasons and deep-pocketed travellers. Prodigals returned would slip back into type, worldly tales outshone by the yarns of local raconteurs. These folks knew what they wanted. They knew what they liked. Wary of outsiders and insular to a fault, they committed to constancy. All else was affront and imprecation.

When the call came in of a domestic disturbance, the initial expectation was of an argument turned ugly. The duty officers who made the inspection kept that view as the property came into sight. It was only when they approached a crudely barred up door that their thoughts wavered. They knocked and called out to those inside. A muffled voice from within bade them to go around the back and gain entry that way. Flashlights at once searching and guiding, they did just that. Finding the door unlocked, they carefully drew it open and moved with praying mantis-like precision. Following voices, they were lured to the living room, where they encountered a scene unlike any they had expected. Bound tight a man and two young ladies crouched in the corner. To their immediate left, near the now cooling hearth, a jagged indent gaped into plaster. Then, when looking down at the cowering, huddled bodies, it became apparent that one had been hit. An officer raced to the victim, uttering words of comfort while her colleague called for an ambulance.

The wound was not fatal. It had nicked the young lady's shoulder before ricocheting into the wall. Blood wept slowly, darkening her checked flannelette shirt. Initial agonies seemed to have subsided, the profusely sweating teen lying almost numb in her waxy, colourless skin. One officer knelt beside her, while the other searched the house. The man of the house, down and defeated, called out from his bondage.

'I wouldn't bother. He left a quarter hour ago.'

'Are you sure?'

'Yeah. Boarded up the front door and then scarpered.'

'You sure it was fifteen minutes ago?'

'Yep. Can see the clock from here and haven't had much to do except check the time.'

'Okay. Well, let me get you out of this tangle and we can find out exactly what happened here.'

A mangled knot of rope and cable ties, the officer could see why struggles to escape had been in vain. It was only with the aid of a Stanley knife and delicate perseverance that the trio were set free. Rubbing their aching wrists–and the wounded child inspecting her throbbing upper arm before they elevated it in a makeshift sling – they hardly knew what to do. The inquisitive officer, returning gun to holster, re-entered the room and confirmed that no one else lurked within.

'He's gone. Looks like he helped himself to a bit of food, but otherwise left the place fairly clean.'

'That's a relief. Did you check all rooms?'

'Yeah, but only a quick scan. We'll need a list of personal effects to know if anything else has been taken.'

As one officer called the station with an update, the other shifted attention to the liberated occupants: a woebegone man and his two shell-shocked daughters. The immediate threat had abated, and consolation was now uppermost in mind. Sitting on furniture instead of the floor, cups of tea were nursed, and a delicate form of questioning begun.

'I know this has been very traumatic for you and we will give you as much time as you need, but we need to find out what happened here tonight.'

His offspring imparting mutual comfort, the father acted as doleful spokesperson.

'I wish I'd done something, fought him, anything.'

'You did well. You're all alive. That may not be the case if you'd acted differently.'

'Yeah, I know. Being overpowered by that lunatic doesn't make me feel like much of a man though.'

'Did you know your attacker?'

'No, never seen him before.'

'Did he seem to recognise you? Do you think he targeted you?'

'Who knows? I don't think he knew us, but he seemed pretty keen to get in.'

'Can you explain the events that took place, going back to the start? Please take your time.'

'Sure. It happened in a flash, but also seemed to take forever. We were sitting here watching TV.'

'Sitting where you are now?'

'Yeah, I was here, with Christy—my eldest—next to me. Jasmine was over where you're sitting.'

'Sorry, please go on.'

'So, we're minding our own business when we heard this massive bang at the front door.'

'Like a knock?'

'Maybe if it was an elephant knocking. More like someone hit it with a battering ram.'

'And then?'

'Before we really had time to think, there was another, louder bang, before the door came crashing down.'

'That must have been quite a shock.'

'Yeah, I hate to swear in front of the girls, but I must admit I let the 'f' word slip, just because of the shock, you know?'

'Of course. I'm sure I would've too. What happened next?'

'It was like time stood still for a moment, but when it started up again this big bloke was standing in the doorway and pointing two guns in our direction.'

'Big bloke? Can you describe him?'

'A big, bushman kind of character, dressed really well but also kind of scruffy.'

'What sort of outfit?'

'A lot of brown and black. Wide-brimmed hat, heavy coat, dark strides. Couldn't see his shoes, but his step was heavy.'

'And his face?'

'Thick beard and hair beneath his hat. Not that I swing that way, but he was alright looking, fairly clean features if you know what I mean.'

'Of course. You got a good look at him?'

'Well, he wasn't hiding or anything, and he spent a bit of time up close, tying us up. Stank a bit too.'

'What of?'

'Like a wet dog smell. You know, like he'd been out in the rain and hadn't really dried properly.'

One daughter interjected, 'And his breath stunk.'

'Oh, of anything in particular?'

'Just of old food, I guess. Not sure he brushed his teeth very much. No way would I be kissing that.'

'So, he entered the room and pointed two guns at you. What happened next?'

'He started talking to us and telling us he just wanted food.'

'Was he aggressive, threatening?'

'Not really. He had a pretty unforgiving tone, if you know what I mean, but he wasn't shouting or anything like that.'

'And, so, you let him have something to eat?'

'Yep, though he didn't want us roaming free. Thought we might make a run or rush him or something.'

'Which is when he tied you up?'

'Yeah.'

'Mr...'

'Blackwell. But call me Adrian, please.'

'Thanks, Adrian. What happened after he tied you up?'

'He wandered around the house. Helped himself to whatever he liked and came back with two bags of stuff.'

'Stuff? Do you have any idea what?'

'Was hard to tell, but mainly food I reckon. Didn't seem interested in much else.'

'You don't think he was looking for anything in particular?'

'He'd be disappointed if he was. Since the wife died there hasn't been much fancy to be found around here.'

'I'm sorry, Adrian.'

As the brow-beaten narrator broke down, sympathy flowed and sold comfort.

'We're nearly done – and the ambulance should be here any minute.'

'I know', he spluttered between tears, 'but it's just been so hard and now this on top of everything else...'

'You've done nothing wrong and you're all safe. You'll be okay. You'll get through this.'

Once a shaky equilibrium had returned, the questioning wound on, until cut short by a van that took all three family members away to be examined. They had endured much. But they had survived. And with clarity and cohesion they had provided the most contemporaneous account of this rogue to date. Now the region's police were reading from the same hymnal script. This intruder, regardless of his fluctuating modus operandi, fit the bill of the local scourge. And now, in the slipstream of a low-calibre slug, a charge of attempted murder could dangle around his neck.

- CHAPTER 10 -

He could not believe he'd shot someone. And a girl at that. He would garner no sympathy that way. Scolding himself for carelessness, even his token reparation of the door could not assuage the guilt. He thought he was a better shot than that, that aiming for wall meant he'd hit wall and nothing else. Maybe she'd budged and shifted into line? He knew that was rationalisation gone mad. More likely, the imp scratching his brain had nudged the barrel far enough left that the warning shot became a skimming blow. Maybe he'd wanted to hit her, to inflict pain? He didn't feel any euphoria afterwards; in fact, he'd bolted from the room to regain comprehension and repress emotion. As he hammered the oaken board closed and shut out frigid winter air, he'd found it impossible not to avert his eyes at intervals to check on his victim. Her cries would haunt him for days (Weeks? Years?) and the sobs of her sister could drown all ambition. He was almost speechless and his swagger ground to a halt. It was all he could do to remember his plunder before departing at breakneck pace, harried by the stern reproach of a bold and unburied ghost.

Revved hotter than a Wilcannia heatwave, the four-wheel drive summoned all its power to catapult from a standstill into the guts of the night. Realising the ferocity with which he'd made his escape, Luke lowered the tempo of his heart and felt the surrounding machine follow suit. There was no point getting busted for speeding. With no fixed abode or destination, he set his sights on driving as far as he could. He wasn't, however, ready to forsake the area that he'd come to call home. He'd stretch its borders and perhaps lie low for a time. But he wasn't running, and he'd sooner hang than admit as much.

Thoughts of the family refused to go away. He had hardly considered his own until now, but the hopelessness and innocence of this clan touched him deeply. He pictured the faces of his mother and father, of the uncle who regaled him with fire in his eyes. He even visualised siblings he never had, knowing that part of him wished this weren't so. He recalled the bond between that man and his daughters, perceptible even in chaos and strife, and he knew, if he'd let it, he'd find the same within. There may never be an easy way, but he vaguely committed to righting this wrong. Misgivings revolved and fluttered around his head; their wings only clipped by the stark finality of his trajectory. His reckless ambition was bruising the lives of others. What had started as a game was having consequences that, while anticipated, cut shockingly deep. It was one thing to envisage what might happen. It was another entirely to endure it and watch it unfold by your hand. Conscience was a restless bedfellow.

Cast out from his self-made Eden, he charted a vertiginous course down a teetering escarpment. Hands trembling at the wheel and then gripping like a vice, he darted under a starry sky, pinpricks in the firmament like accusatory progenitors of inquisition. Oncoming headlights were rare and quick to taper in peripheral sight. He flicked on the radio to distract his thoughts, scrolling through channels to settle on something that might sooth. Easy listening stations were anything but, while the drone of talkback drove daggers into his skull. Mundane as it was, a news service was as good as it got, but then he waited for the sound of his name and turned off the noise in disgust. The remaining drive was silent, with only cat's eyes and guilt for company.

Wayward in a timeless void, it was only the roadblock of exhaustion that brought him to a halt. Luke broke free of the highway's hypnotic spell and pulled up at a desolate rest area. He got out of the car, walked to the back, and opened the door on his hotel for the night. Cramped as it was, a nest of well-used bedding made for cosy, almost seductive, confines. While nocturnal mysteries played out in situ, the ungainly limbs of this ravened beast sought space like a leech seeking life-flow. More fatigued than he realised, as his eyes closed, he was transported to another world of no quick return. Relief bathed his sins and sutured weeping wounds. They would open again, but for now, they could heal uninfected.

The next morning, mouth dust-dry and head pulsating, he exited his spelaean abode and sat on a bench gulping draughts of country air. He squinted, irritated by the gentle morning sun, and kicked stones in the dirt. He focused on thought, but his thoughts made little sense. Putting some of this down to hunger, Luke re-joined the highway and continued south. Arriving in Holbrook and dressing to blend in, he found a café and placed his order. Never mind that he had supplies in abundance; it felt important to lash out and disrupt his cycle of existence. Alert and furtive at first, he gradually relaxed over a hot cup of coffee and let cares slip away. When breakfast neared, he could taste it before he saw it. Smoky bacon, fried eggs, sausage, mushrooms, herb-grilled tomato, a hash brown and thick-cut sourdough toast steamed from the plate and called to his palate. The aroma was an opiate shooting sparks in his brain. As the comingling flavours erupted through his system, it triggered a semblance of contentment that shadowed him out the door.

If suspicion's risk brooked no favours, it motivated politeness. Not that Luke's manners had ever been deficient (shooting girls aside), but they were now effusive to an elaborate degree: a medley of 'pleases', 'thank yous' and 'good mornings' delivered with a beaming smile and conspicuous intent to assist. It was as if through performances of social submission, he hoped to achieve atonement. Feeling fat as a Christmas turkey and twice as stuffed, he returned to his car, idled for a minute and then eased into the sparse flow of local traffic. He loved these country towns with their innocence and time-trapped honesty. He wondered why he'd ever craved the spotlight, when to slip in and out of town unnoticed now seemed the height of desirability. Do nothing to draw attention and you'll invariably hanker for it; feel the light shine on unsavoury deeds and you'll flog off your soul to avoid it. With that in mind, he drove on, seeking the embrace of another secluded country town.

Sneaking up on the state border, he tried the radio again and found distraction instead of exasperation. The news of the world seemed so trivial; a man who had retired from society's throe found its beliefs incongruous, its ambitions immoral. The scandals that enraptured others were of no consequence to him. It was purely for the metronomic patter of the newsreader's delivery that he continued to listen. It was a fitting soundtrack to the clockwork rhythms of the road and the monotony of passing scenery. Farmlands sprawled, undulating grey and green-tinged in pursuit of coming spring. Sheep and cattle dotted the hills with the sole intent of nourishment, marbling rich through their fattening bellies. Fences taut and fences loose strung endless chains of demarcation. And a feeble sun barely reached the earth, this quilt-work of pastures with a swathe of bitumen down the middle, from one breached horizon to the next.

After bridging the Murray, he swung to the left. He felt as though he'd made an escape, as a complaisant exile from a land that was never his own. He wasn't stupid enough to think the Victorian police wouldn't speak to their neighbours and mobilise against him, but there was more chance of breathing space down here. That's all he wanted–to gather his thoughts and vanish for a while, like Flash

Johnny Gilbert in pixie-like flight. As hands struck the hour and a bulletin begun, this felt within reach.

> *'Police are searching for a man believed responsible for a home invasion in country New South Wales in which a 14-year old girl was shot in the arm. The incident took place outside the Central West town of Oberon around 8:30 last night. The girl, along with her father and sister, were tied up while the intruder ransacked the house, before leaving them bound on the floor. The suspect is described as a Caucasian male, around 180 centimetres tall, medium build, heavily bearded and dressed in the manner of a bushman. He is believed to be armed. The public are advised to exhibit caution before approaching anyone fitting this description. The family members are in Bathurst Hospital for observation and the girl's injury is not considered life-threatening. Anyone with information is requested to contact Crime Stoppers'*

Luke's jaw dropped. And then the perimeter of his mouth lit up in a smile. His senses aflame, he pulled to the side of the road, nearly swiping another car. His own car skidded to a stop in a puff of dust. Thrust forward in his seat, his hands clenched the wheel and then all he could hear was his heartbeat. Then came the deluge of thoughts. And the realisation, sounding like a chime, as clear as a bell. He'd achieved renown. He was a man of danger, to be 'cautiously approached'. Despite their crippling terror, his victims had shown admirable attention to detail. He bristled slightly at the suggestion he merely dressed in 'the manner of' a bushman, but these witnesses were not privy to his outdoor acumen. He reclined in his seat and beamed like a Cheshire cat. After weeks of solitude and internalisation, to hear himself spoken about was to re-join humankind, in altered form.

Dizzied by this unexpected invocation, Luke was shaken on his course. There was nothing to say this was the first exposure of his identity, though it was the first he was aware of. In that regard and in its method of deliverance, fate had been merciful. What happened from here was anyone's guess, though he had a say in that. He watched a stream of aloof brethren pass by and quelled the impulse to bellow, 'It's me! I'm the man they're after!'. They'd stall in bemusement or continue unabated to destinations known or unknown, distant or proximate. But he could find them if he wanted and could take them if he dared.

The road from here constricted fast. Like a tobacco addict's arteries, it was clogging tar and thrombotic menace. It would slice through mountain landscapes in which he could get lost: great snow-capped peaks, inhospitable and bold; jutting ridges and steepling cliffs; uncharted valleys where brumbies foal; alpine creeks spilt from vernal thaw, feeding trout-thick rivers on tumbling flow; abandoned huts in wind-battered pockets of plaintive salvation; limestone shawls and subterranean boughs, luring with shelter to asphyxiant slumber. If he chose to, he might fade from view and shape shift into memory. For all its imperfections, the modern world could be quick to forget.

Later that day, in crepuscular review, held in a trance by the fierce lapping flames, he burrowed within and found purpose unchanged.

Owens had long ago grown used to receiving unsavoury news at inopportune times. Nature had called moments before his colleagues from Oberon, and the news that sifted through cut short his ablutions. With half-wet hands, his phone was like a cake of soap, and it was all he could do to reach for a towel and pat himself dry. The night was by now pot-bellied and sated, yet it somehow held appetite for more. The report itself was no shock to the system:

there'd been an armed home invasion just out of Oberon; a man and his two daughters bound and one girl shot a glancing blow to the upper arm; the alleged perpetrator, a spitting image of you-know-who. The last part was achingly familiar. Even the preceding details, as severe as they were, followed the discernible pattern of inconsistency that had become an egregious calling card.

The line went dead and words hung like bedsheets on an old Hills Hoist. Owens gathered his thoughts in the mirror's brawling vortex. At risk of devaluing a young girl's health, any news was good news and fresh news was, in this caper, worth its weight in diamonds. That this renegade remained active made him easier to catch. That he was broadening his portfolio knotted more ropes to hang him with. That he fled on four wheels sketched contours of the chase. And yet, the lack of vision smudged lines that frenzied sound had made. Cursing this one lapse of serendipity, Owens knew there was digging to be done. Prior notice was fine, but there was a need to know what they were looking for. By the time the cat was out, the rat may well be down the drainpipe.

Phone to one ear and his wife in the other, Owens started circling wagons. His Oberon associates had played their part, spreading a description of the suspect to all but the farthest-flung crevices of the state. Surely there were enough cameras out there that he'd be spotted, filling up with petrol, stalking the aisles of a supermarket or rearranging his trousers. The advantages by which this scoundrel's predecessors flourished had been stripped from twenty-first century citizenry. And based on what he knew of Australian history, Owens had deep-seated confidence that modern troopers were a far more capable adversary than those of colonial times. Blind Freddy himself (baronet of the realm, hunter of outlaws, his bullet-blown body weltering intestate) could see that. Inchoate and ill-equipped, they'd been a hapless cluster of strut and bluster, men of substance undermined by a system almost designed to fail. Though imbued with noble spirits, their tools were substandard, and their wits dulled as by pumice. They'd be awarded a medal for merely catching a fever. Deliver a killer to their doorstep and they'd climb out the window.

Owens settled quickly into character, slipped out the door and was soon on his way into town. There was an eerie countenance to the late-night streets; lamplit and noiseless, they brooded like shrines. Passing through, Owens almost felt like he was on parade. He arrived at the station, parked his car and stepped into caliginous surrounds. It was bitingly cold, but more temperate than the atmosphere he'd come from. Pacing towards the promise of warmth, he lingered at the sound of company: a junior officer fulfilling her end of a thankless bargain, dragged to the station from a coy yet promising date. He remembered those days like they were yesterday, while knowing they were anything but.

It is often from intimate gatherings that monumental events take shape. As the Senior Sergeant prepared to address his troops, he prayed this would again be the case. He waited for his coterie to find seats within the drab yet functional meeting room and then took centre stage.

'Right, thank you all for coming in this late in the evening. I know we'd all much rather be curled up in our beds.'

An acquiescent murmur confirmed the point.

'As you've all heard, things with our wannabe bushranger have taken a bit of a turn. He stormed a house in Oberon tonight and a young girl, a young lady, was shot. Fortunately, whether by good luck or good management, she will be okay. But it makes it vital that we apprehend this bugger pronto, before he does any more damage.

'First things first, I think it's important we look at what we know and what is probable. You all know a bit about this case by now and have no doubt formed an impression of the bloke we're after.

'Based on the description given to Oberon cops—and it was a detailed description, as they have pretty much all been—it's 99%

certain we're dealing with the same man. Appearance and demeanour are consistent with what we've encountered before. The only material difference has been in the crimes. So, I think it's safe to assume that the bloke who carried out those car-jackings, who held up the pub, who desecrated Ben Hall's grave and who's stolen various effects from around the area is also responsible for this incident. Does anyone think otherwise?'

'Maybe it's an imitator, Sarge?'

'Always possible, but let's say it's unlikely. I'm not sure this Barclay character is well-known enough yet to be inspiring others.

'So, assuming this is him, we need to look at the facts of this case. We know that he bound this family and shot the girl. Do we think he intended to shoot her, or was it an accident?'

'Might have been a warning shot? He would've known the blow was unlikely to kill her and he didn't follow up, so either he was disturbed and scarpered, or he didn't mean to take a life.'

'Good point, McKay. When you consider that he took the time to board up the front door, he wasn't in a rush. So we can discount him being disturbed. Does anyone think he intended to kill this girl?'

Heads shook in unison.

'Neither do I. I think he either panicked, or it was a warning, either intended to hit as it did, or to penetrate the wall.'

'Do you think he would panic though Sarge? With the family tied up and no one nearby, he should have felt fairly controlled?'

'That's true. But while he seems to have a fairly even temper, there have been flashes of rage. Like many crims, he appears to crave being in control and can lash out when he feels that control threatened. But yes, I agree that was probably not the case.

'So, let's say it was a warning. The question then is if he intended to hit the girl or not. Any thoughts? And I should say, the girl and her family weren't sure about intent.'

'Do you think it matters? I mean, either he targeted the girl and hit her, or he aimed for the wall and missed.'

'Or his gun went off by accident.'

'Which is all possible. I guess what I think is most important is how he might have felt after he did this. If he didn't intend to hit the girl–either aiming for the wall or his gun going off of its own accord–then it probably came as a shock. And even if he aimed for her, assuming he's never put a bullet in someone before he probably didn't feel great.'

'Not great enough to board up a broken door before he left?'

'That's right.'

'Displays a level of composure though, doesn't it?'

'It does. Composure mixed with guilt. I think he shocked himself by his actions and felt like making a token effort to repair the damage he'd caused.'

'He could've called an ambulance or something if he wanted to do that.'

'And that may have crossed his mind. But I guess he figured she'd be okay and that calling an emergency service would do him no favours.'

Pausing for breath and a sip of coffee, the chairman shuffled his papers.

'So, are we all on the same page here?'

'Sure are.'

'Too right.'

'Bloody oath.'

'Great. Now we need to find this arsehole. Connors, what did our colleagues tell us about his mode of escape?'

'Well, he left in a vehicle, and not one that belonged to the inhabitants, which would suggest he drove the same one to the house.'

'Any sightings? Description?'

'Not yet. Frustratingly, the family couldn't see it from inside the house. Oberon cops plan to question more locals in the morning. There were tyre marks though, and the father did describe the sound of the engine.'

'How did he describe it?'

'Like a rocket launching into orbit.'

'Sounds like we need to get police on Mars looking out for him.'

'If only. He's still our problem until I hear otherwise. The tyre marks: did they tell us anything?'

'It's a four-wheel drive—and obviously a powerful one based on the audio evidence.'

'Good. Apart from anything else we need to check for any four-wheel drives – or 'SUVs' for the city wankers out there – stolen in recent times. As he has never owned his own vehicle, has no fixed address and was last seen riding a horse, chances are this is a recent acquisition. Find the car and we can track him, no matter where he's gone.

'We now have cops across the state watching this bloke like a hawk. Chances are he's still nearby, but after this drama he may wish to cool his heels for a while. To him, that means going bush, which makes it tough but not impossible to find him.

'This is no doubt about to get a lot more press, especially when the news-people put two and two together. We are also likely to cop some heat from the big smoke. This bloke is still more a nuisance than a nightmare, but the longer it takes to catch him the worse we look and the more pressure there will be for city cops to intervene. I don't want that to happen. As far as I'm concerned, there are no finer men and women in the land than you lot sitting before me. No one knows this area like us, no one feels its heartbeat, no one knows its nooks and crannies, no one understands its people and its pressures. This man has transgressed on our turf. And, as sons and daughters of this turf, we will get the better of him. He's come from the outside and attacked our liberty, drunk on some kind of twisted historical re-enactment. But he didn't account for us. We're strong, we're united, we're smart and we're determined. If we work together, then he's more than met his match.'

Owens, almost enervated, scanned his audience for the spark of recognition. Their faces said it all. No words could be spoken to hammer the message home more.

'Thanks team. Those of you off-duty, get some rest and we'll get stuck in again in the morning. And let's hope for no more news between now and then.'

As the rest of the team returned to warm and welcoming lodgings, Owens felt ready to commence the hunt that instant, to find this villain and throttle him. It was only a voice of reason from within that held him in check. Instead, being careful to pull sheets back gently, he climbed into bed with the restless dark and attempted to drift into sleep. Charged as he was from the evening's meeting, the agitated stirring of a woken wife barely caught his attention.

- CHAPTER 11 -

When Blaxland, Lawson and Wentworth trudged, with exploratory intent, from the fringe of settlement, across emu-speckled plains, fording broad Nepean to the furthermost shore, scaling cobalt ramparts to mysteries beyond and cresting forested plateaux propped on sheer sandstone foundations, they mollified their exertions with the best-watered country of any they'd seen. When those waters turned gold nearly thirty years hence, the complexion of the colony changed forever. An influx of desperados and towns built around them (erected on promise and mired in dysentery) deposited slag in the craw of tradition. A century and a half down this adamantine track, the towns were less vibrant, but the hoodlums still came.

Crotchety and deprived of rest, the flinty Senior Sergeant was in no mood for romanticised history when he reported for duty the following morning. His sleep had been tormented by dreams, stentorian and incessant. They swarmed like hornets and drained with their sting. He awoke off-kilter and not quite himself, but the cogs within still turned. Tensions at home, sly in their awakening, had ameliorated overnight, and he arose to a peck on the cheek and a piping hot breakfast. This was more than a token gesture and his addled brain knew it. This was reassurance and a pledge to stay the course, but it also felt like approval's touch on a shoulder bent to the wheel. He expected no such gestures from his kids: barring requests for money and the odd query about the evolving case they were increasingly detached. The trials of life left him helpless to prevent this. They could deal with their mother–and with him in due course.

It was not until his third espresso that Owens felt human again. His glassy, blood-cracked eyes scrolled through paper after paper, one computerised image after another, with nothing registering but the clamour in his head. He was trying to think his way through a labyrinth of data, to drill into the mindset of this perplexing offender, yet how could he step into another man's mind when he could not escape his own? And then, how could he comprehend something that curried no reason? He'd spent a lifetime plumbing the depths of the criminal mind: the sociopath bred, the miscreant born, the abused and mistreated, doggone and defeated, the easily led and impossible to tame. They'd all shown their faces and he felt acquainted to a degree, attuned to their nuances and reprehensible mores. This man seemed to have everything going for him. A loving, stable family unit, no financial stress, no known issues with addiction or debasement, no train of influence to run him off the rails. And perhaps that touched on the problem's crux, even though the fug in Owens' brain disallowed him to realise it. Far from being led astray by the sins of others, this compulsion to trespass had grown rampant as ivy for want of impression from those outside. This man had gone to great lengths to block the outside world from his view, or at least any part he disliked. If jellyfish slept wrapped in their deadly threads, there'd be little wonder that the waters around were clouded with poison.

Having nurtured his prejudices to the exclusion of all others, it made sense that Barclay's thoughts were askew, even if it couldn't explain his actions.

Owens had just risen for a head-clearing walk when news came in to blow the cobwebs out.

'Boss, looks like we might have found the car-well, not quite found it, but at least we have an idea of what he's driving.'

'Really? This could be the best break we've had in ages. What's the story?'

'A lady from out of Forbes called this morning. Says she and her hubbie were away for a couple of weeks and returned to find their Pajero missing.'

'Which doesn't tell us when it went missing, but it fits in with where we expect our suspect acquired new transport.'

'That's right. It's not a million miles from where the horse was found. We actually visited the house after we found the horse, but with no one home we–and the neighbours we spoke to–assumed the car was on holiday with its owners.'

'Fair enough too. You have full details of the vehicle?'

'Already memorised like a PIN number.'

'Doesn't fill me with much confidence: I'm hopeless with them.'

'Don't need to worry with this. We have the details and we're circulating them to all stations. We're also checking cameras near of Forbes, Oberon and all points in between.'

'Might see things on those that will scar you for life.'

'No doubt. But hopefully there's footage of this bloke.'

'That's what I'm worried about.'

- CHAPTER 12 -

Kelly Country: a blood-run of emerald pride and dishevelled yet proud resistance. Pristine wilderness dotted with smoking campfires and the clanging of a makeshift forge. The name was a clarion call for the patriot within, the downtrodden and defiant, the Reaper's flock in perpetual toil. From gaudy tropes and trinkets glared that imposing pig-iron visor, bemusing in its journey from carapace to kitsch. Around it wove a confused, conflicting history, semi-literate and open to wide interpretation. To some it defined the nation; to others it was an abiding mark of shame. In a land where pedestals are made to be burned, this towering scaffold had instead been reinforced and the gibbet declaration subsumed into lore.

Luke tipped the dregs from his billy onto the smouldering pit before him. He buttered the remaining damper and clasped it in his mouth while he set about packing up camp. Cockatoos screeched overhead like a deployment of Spitfire bombers, never resigned to the finality of their mission. Supplies were plentiful, but his appetite was spartan. As lemon-toned sabres of morning lambency pierced the sky and atomised into the tranquil glade below, hope was abundant, and doom had no name. There were countless places like this that could harbour a man for decades. Leave these lands to the government and they'd see the earth singed; give them to the poacher and he'd make the desert sing. As Luke eased away into eddies unknowable, this tuneful inheritance brought the Wild Colonial Boy's song to his lips.

Like a country town lolly shop, the names evoked magic and sensations of yore: Greta, Benalla, Violet Town, Mansfield, Euroa and terminus Glenrowan. Each told its own story as part of a legend; fact conflated fiction in an omnibus of romantic sprawl. Reality had faint hope of competing, yet the bushranging spirit is a pugnacious beast. Tactile and adjacent, it was too much to resist. Purloined wheels rolled down walnut-fringed roads, swerving past roadkill and ravens at feast. With time to kill and distance in hand, a brief detour was nothing to ask. In his twenty-four and a half years he'd never been this far south (not physically, at least); a familial anomaly of top-end imbalance. And yet, stranger though he was, it felt so familiar, so redolent of home. He was a prodigal son to soil un-explored and it made him almost blind to the danger.

Visualising himself scything down a dust-encrusted thoroughfare, hands at the reins of a Cobb and Co charger instead of grasping the steering wheel of a car, the muddle of portent was thick in his veins and the eyes of the law were like the buzzing of flies. In the scene's majesty and the power it infused, a cloak of invincibility draped his brawny shoulders. 'This', he intoned, breath rank and unshared, 'is my destiny', stooping to stereotype over substance. Savant of the golden age, he should have known better.

The town of Greta held muted fulfilment in its stringy arms, an aura unmatched by laconic exposition. The Kelly clan's ruins stood picaresque and disinterested. The streets kept their secrets untold, but to walk them was to retrace steps of the pantheon. To drive away was both relief and reward.

He cleaved the King Valley and surfaced in Mansfield, buttressed by mountains and teaming with life. Destiny stumbled in the face of a crowd. Febrile with timorous energy, he skirted the throng of skiers, boarders and weekend marauders, the riotous tintinnabulation of alarm bells like a sledgehammer to his ears. His reaction was swift: a squealing U-turn just before the main street. A police car cruised past, and the sledgehammer hit harder. Thoughts were in frenzy and an entire town, tumescent in winter robes, seemed out to bear witness. Stop signs jumped out like byway bandits and traffic thickened when willed to subside. It was a nightmarish getaway, interminable and stifling. Had his cognition been so inclined, it may have drawn parallels to escape from robbery at arms, albeit de-fleshed of its pernicious threat. Instead, once loosed from fetters and licking his wounds, they memorialised the incident as a cautionary tale, an errant adjunct to a greater recital. Roads no longer led to Glenrowan. As though ringed by bushfire, this sleepy hamlet was now strictly off limits. Nothing had *really* happened, yet anxieties within insisted they had, that walls were closing in and flambeaux-carrying mobs were converging on this goat-tracked interior, chanting and damning his name. State lines like boundary wire were no imposition. Technology's spinnerets, unseen and insidious, entrapped men in ways his forebears never dreamed. Hawk eyes were piercing, beaks curved and twitching. He needed to be smarter. No more flights of fancy or genuflection at the feet of antiquity. No more death-wish missions for a peek through peepholes torn. At the side of the road, cars rushing by, map on his knees and index finger hovering like a kite, he settled on a track more obscure, less expected. He turned on the radio, impatient for sound, and as sonorous melodies flitted and flared, he looked down upon himself and foundered in confusion.

He didn't realise he'd fallen asleep. When he awoke, it was to a twilit panorama that inveigled him to push on. His neck had a crick and his mouth was bone-dry. He switched off the radio, then dug round for a flask of water and a paltry meal of cheese and biscuits, massaging his neck with a spare hand while pondering the absurdity of his situation. He was nowhere and no one, an amateur outlaw with a pitiful, pockmarked body of work. He'd done enough to be in trouble, but nowhere near enough to be immortal. Did he even have that in him? Was he really the killing kind? Not that hands clean of blood couldn't shake the trees of history. Ben Hall never killed. Wronged and dispossessed, he did however reap a mighty whirlwind, a snarling storm of vengeance, stoked by local fervour and couched in genteel terms. He was a man who prodded, poked and at his wits' end, drank deep the scent of the land and the times. But they were his times, not Luke's, and the maudlin bandit knew it. He'd tried, but that scent was not his to ingest. And any wrongs done to him bore the mark of his own creation.

Alone again, phantasms at peace, he scythed through the dark like a blade. Hulking peaks sneered, guarding the way like trolls with their gold. The bush was a mass of manifold parts that yielded and blocked, brooking no trespass but permitting a narrow course. Yellow diamonds of warning stippled that course, but their hazards were none that could trouble him now. These roads begat rivers of rage and remorse. And through it all, his mind was in quicksand, clutching for anything stable and sure.

He passed through towns of ephemeral splendour, mined until calcified ribs baked like clay. In night's maturation they simpered as one. They lured as Sirens and passed like a stone, straining, uncomfortable and greased with relief. He thought of the people who lived in these outposts and as a son of the city, he could never understand. He wondered what they'd think of a rat in the galley if he dropped anchor and rested for a while. Would they welcome a stranger and not ask or be told? Would they turn a blind eye if suspicion arose? Or would homespun charm crumble under moral duress? If accepted, could he be trusted not to prey on those who sheltered? He may be no orphan of lupine litter, but he'd studied the ways of the wolf in such depth that to lower his hackles and sheath his fangs may no longer be a matter of will.

In one town he set both beacon and decoy, ditching his transport, removing the plates and buying another. The tank nearly empty, he drained reserves of petrol under lunar supervision. From here, the road staggered on in alpine suspension, until teasingly, it plotted descent. Brake–pads like griddle irons slammed at each bend, echoing through valleys with the shrieks of a harpy. Traffic was light and progress, while jarring, was steady. Nocturnal surveillance was nowhere to be found. The Central West was worlds away and felt even further removed. As slopes cascaded and petered out into foothills, a weight left his shoulders and breath returned to burning lungs. Lights in the distance now brought optimism, not dread. In a land of no borders he felt he'd crossed a trenchant line. A steel tidal grip pulled him on towards the coast and like an outback child on virgin shores found sheer intoxication in the salty blow. Approaching witching hour, bedazzled by spell, he drank of the ocean air and scavenged, like a hermit crab, for a home in which to dwell.

The pub was heaving in Friday night glory, boisterous with laughter and the clinking of glasses. Rugby league blared from a screen in the corner, prompting bellows and curses and good–natured ribbing. Pool cues struck with a chalky caress, while poker machines flashed like carnival rides. The beer garden wafted with cigarettes and bawdy humour, blue smoke and blue jokes swirling into the night. A fluid stream of patrons walked from post to bar and back, each time a little bolder and each path a little shakier. If a tee–totalling cop seemed a fish out of water, here he felt like a shark atop Ayer's Rock. And he held court before the crapulous mass as he cleared his throat and spoke in valediction.

'Excuse me, everyone. Bit of shoosh, please.'

What he got was as good as expected. He tapped a glass with a key and called for more silence.

'Thank you. Now, as you know, after nearly five years with us, Constable McKay is leaving us to move to the big smoke.'

Howls of derision burst from smiling faces, and those in proximity gave hefty pats on the back.

'Some might suggest she should see a shrink instead, but that's her choice and maybe they all considered her too far gone for help. While we will miss you terribly, I think I speak for all of us in saying that Kelly, we wish you all the best in your new posting.'

'Hear, hear!'

'Too bloody right!'

'Show those fuckwits how it's done, Kel!'

'From all of us–and I'm sure from everyone else you've worked with at this station over the years–thank you for the tireless efforts and good humour you've put into your policing. You're a credit to yourself and to your family –'

'–And a bloody good sort! –'

'–and it looks like you'll be missed in other ways.'

Wolf whistles signified agreement.

'So, Kelly, go well and prosper. I'm sure we'll miss you more than you'll miss this unruly mob of dickheads.'

'Cheers!'

Not bred for blushing, the sentiment nonetheless affected the departing officer. Her response was gracious and uninterrupted, fading away in more toasts to her health. His duty concluded, Owens retreated to the shadows, suspending judgment yet watchful and tense. As soon as decorum permitted, he was out the door and cursing the night for its cold.

The next morning, sober buoy on a queasy sea, he berthed at the station and knuckled down to work. Reports had come in of sightings–some north, some south, some east and some west. Each had to be dealt with, though all were not equal: a gun-metal Pajero in Mudgee raised hopes, until a mother and quartet of kids came on board. Two days and three nights had passed since the shooting, and while treads in the mud had done much to confirm, this fiend's exact whereabouts were shrouded in mist. Southbound from Oberon was logical terrain; there were open roads with detours aplenty, providing retreat north or west, while they forsook the east, beyond all return. As for deep down below, beneath the clods of porous soil, the Devil seemed unlikely to be ready for this miasma.

A call was placed to Belfield in case there'd been a message home, but that drawn and forlorn couple only shared his desperation. Acquaintances and distant friends were sounded out for information; their fuzzy responses implied collusion until common sense deemed them amaurotic as their inquisitors. Pressure from the media was building, craving fodder for an insatiable news cycle. In a world of quick results and the standard half-cocked apportionment of blame, this was a black mark oozing within. Heat was coming from the capital, with questions posed in less than empathetic terms. Where was the suspect? Why hadn't they found him? What was being done to secure an arrest? Were these country cops up to the task? This one loose cannon, this time-warped revivalist, had become a lance in sensitive flesh.

As he again pored over details of the case, he gazed at the image of the wanted man. This was a portrait of innocence, pristine and idealised, yet he knew it masked uncomfortable truths; that he couldn't put a finger on them was far from the least. He studied the posture, the look of alertness, and drilled down, hoping to find darker shades beneath. What the parents couldn't see, as far as he could tell, surely his experience was better equipped to find. While that couple was sweet, if undoubtedly naïve, without their clouded loyalties he would always be at an advantage.

As he went to pull away from the photo, the faces of his own children flashed before his eyes. They took on the pose and visage of young Barclay, while subtly snarling and baring their teeth. He turned over the image, yet the faces remained, hinting at something unsightly and malign. It startled him. If he thought he knew his children before, recent events threw that into question. How was he better placed than those parents in Belfield? He sought to focus on the faces before him, to seek an answer at their quivering core, yet the images now turned grey scale, cross-hatched and faint. Owens struggled for clarity, for colour to return, yet the more he focused the fainter they became. Then they vanished, and he panicked, storming out the door in cyclonic tribulation. Bloodshot vision followed his path until the screeching of tyres roared away from the kerb. When dust came to rest and ears ceased to ring, the feather-soft drumbeat of life kept thumping away.

He had every intention of heading straight home, of hugging his kids and wife until they were nearly purple, of asking about their feelings, their dreams and concerns, of listening, and nodding, and acutely interacting. He wanted to batter down doors that felt locked. He rued the air of disconnect that threatened to white-ant the foundations of his family and to open a fissure that might swallow them whole. It all seemed clear, so easily resolved, yet he couldn't quite grasp the means of attainment. Conflicting thoughts fulminated in his mind, taking charge of steering as a left turn took the place of a right. The spectre of conflict and difficult conversations, so easy to deal with in a professional sense, was anything but simple when close to the bone. He wasn't ready for it and if he ever had been, he couldn't recall. He cruised familiar streets on an unfamiliar course, thoughts in turmoil and clarity lost. A neon sign flickered and glimmered in the drizzling rain. Owens parked his car and looked at the cheap lettering. As he stepped onto the footpath, the noise in his head was a din. He drew his jacket close and glanced around, unsure of his bearings. He entered a corner building and as he closed the door behind, the demons that dogged him rushed to push in.

'What would you like, mate?'

'Just a coke, thanks. No, bugger it–can you put a dash of bourbon in it?'

'Sure thing.'

The shame was worse than the hangover. Not that the hangover was anything less than a jackhammer staving his skull, but mortification sent him to a special hell. Stricken by a spiritual palsy, he pried apart unwilling eyes and let raw penance flood within. Comprehension took some time, then it hit like a wrecking ball fitted with spikes. He was lying in the corner of his office. His clothes stank. His phone was flat and his wallet empty. Or were those emotions flat and spirit empty? Flatness and emptiness were pervasive. At length, he levered himself from the carpet and up to his chair. His fingers jarred against inflamed temples, and he closed his eyes as flashbacks shot like meteors through his brain. And then he scrambled out of his chair and down the hall to purge all that he was able.

As his phone returned to power, a flurry of messages and missed calls jostled in. He didn't need to read them to know their content, to capture the snowballing tone of concern. And he didn't feel like responding, but he knew that duty must; he'd been derelict in duty once and that was more than enough. He quaffed a hearty gust of air, straightened his posture and chose remorse as his mantra.

'What the hell happened to you last night?'

'I'm sorry.'

'I'm sure you are. You worried us sick. Why didn't you answer your phone?'

'It went flat, and I didn't have a charger.'

'Well, I'm glad you're okay. That's the main thing. What happened last night anyway?'

'I got caught up at the station. I thought I had a charger, and I didn't—until McKay came in this morning—'

'—I thought she finished on Friday? Isn't that why you were out after work?'

'She did, but she had to pick up some things before leaving.'

'And she brought in a phone charger?'

'It was one of the things she needed to pick up. Again, I'm sorry I didn't call. I was stuck at the office and time got away from me—'

'—You didn't think to call from your work phone or, you know, come home?'

'I got stuck with this case. There's a lot happening at the moment and I needed to go through a lot of boring documents here.'

'That you couldn't leave? Steve, that sounds like rubbish.'

He had no response.

'What's going on? Are you having a fling with that officer? Is that what it is?'

His tongue was tied.

'I'd like to know, because it's just not normal for a husband to be out on a Saturday night without telling his wife. Especially one who doesn't drink.'

'Yeah, but what about one who does?'

'Excuse me?'

'If you must know, I freaked out yesterday. It's never happened before, but the pressure of the case, stresses at home—'

'—What stresses at home? If there's a problem, tell me about it.'

'I don't want to go into it now, but you've been difficult to talk to recently.'

'Me? Difficult to talk to? What planet are you living on?'

'Look, I'm heading home now. Can we talk about it then?'

'Yes, we can. But I want to know what you got up to last n—'

'–I had a drink, okay? I went to the pub, and I had a drink. By myself. And you know what? It felt good at the time, but now it feels like shit. I was embarrassed and didn't want you to know. I feel like a complete idiot'

It was her turn to freeze.

'I don't know what came over me, whether being at the pub the night before–sober–planted a seed in my head, or something else. I didn't intend to have a drink, but I did.'

'You drank... alcohol? How much, exactly?'

'It was probably about six bourbon and cokes. I don't think I handled them very well. From what I remember, the bartender seemed almost amused by me.'

'Some sense of humour. I really wish you'd told me what you were doing.'

'Yeah.'

'I am upset with you, but I'm also concerned. Unless you've been hiding something from me, I'm–'

'–I've been hiding nothing, I promise. It's just that I needed a release and lost my mind.'

'You sure did.'

He'd also lost the ability to fight.

'Come home, get yourself tidied up and we'll talk more about this later. Are you okay to drive?'

'I think so. Can always test myself before jumping in the car.'

'Okay. I need you to mow the lawn today, so hopefully you can handle the petrol fumes and exercise without getting sick.'

'That's touch and go at the moment, I'd say. I'd kill for a shower and lie down before anything else.'

'Where did you sleep last night, out of interest?'

'More an alcoholic coma than proper sleep, but there's a patch of carpet in the office's corner with my sweat on it.'

'Oh dear.'

'Not exactly luxury, I know.'

'Sometimes I wonder if you're the same man I married.'

'Yeah. For better or for worse though, I think I am.'

'Then you'd better tell me more about who you are, because I'm not sure I know, and I want no more surprises like this.'

'Yeah. Um, I'd better get home. If I leave now, I'll be home in fifteen.'

'Okay. Drive safe, you big dufus.'

And he did. At least ten kilometres per hour below the speed limit. If one of his brethren had played interceptor, the route of his orbit would have swung back to source.

As he crawled up the drive, deflated yet curiously defiant. Misreading mild placation in his wife's parting tones, he expected a withering scowl and brimstone extracted from the deepest sulphur pits. Instead, he was met with stony-faced disappointment. When the silence broke, it was the strains of apology's coda that resounded through to birth.

'I'm still in shock.'

'I know. So am I.'

'What I don't understand is why you didn't tell me you weren't coming home. You worried me sick.'

'I know. You told me that before. I wish I could explain. I had every intention of telling you, but like the intention to head straight home it just never happened. It's like I momentarily lost my mind.'

'Yeah, you said that before too. I'm not sure what that means. Is this something I should expect to happen again? If it is, make other living arrangements, because I'm not sure I can handle it.'

'What's that supposed to mean?'

'It means what I said: I don't want you doing this again. Is that reasonable enough to expect?'

'Of course it is. Trust me, I feel so horrible that there's no way I'll be putting either of us—or the kids—through that again.'

'And you promise you were there by yourself? There aren't any more secrets I should know?'

'Promise. Apart from random barflies, it was just me and my poor decisions.'

She stared into her husband's eyes and took a moment to gather thoughts.

'Steve, I'm worried about you. This is so out of character and so against everything you believe in. Do you think you should see someone? A shrink maybe?'

'No, I'll be fine. I think I just needed to let off some steam.'

'Well, you sure did that. Just do me a favour and let it off some other way next time.'

As the final curt refrain hung suspended in the air, it felt as though a little had been resolved. As Owens climbed stairs to the master bedroom, he realised that tenuous peace brings less comfort than furious conflict. He removed his rancid clothes and clambered into the shower. Laved by jets of icy atonement, he never heard the footsteps come and whisk those clothes away.

- CHAPTER 13-

Sunrise over the Tasman Sea glowed like treacle poured on velvet. Feet up on a solid oak coffee table. This was living the dream. Luke had stumbled on a beachfront abode with floor to ceiling windows and a sweeping, turquoise vista. It wasn't quite the dingy hideaway to which he'd normally be drawn. Access was less troublesome than expected and the cover of night had been accomplice *par excellence*. Wearied from his travels, he'd slept a few hours before sun had its way, blasting through those salt-crusted panes. He thought of the mornings in desolate clearings, of similar wake-up calls altogether different. He thought of the birds chirping courtship and wisdom. He remembered the rustle of eucalypt leaves and the sweet olfactory balm as they mingled and swirled. He saw dusky wallabies bending to feed, then staring like hypnotists locked to his sight. Right at this moment, as much as it compromised the chart of his existence, he would give up all of that for a lengthy sojourn here.

While cupboards were relatively bare, supplies remained, and the array of cooking implements was a luxury worth exploring. Not that Luke metamorphosed into a gourmand. Stale bread, a tinned bean mix, canned tomatoes and frozen chips would win no votes in a cooking competition—but it was a delicious change from the campfire grill. To eat off crockery and drink from glass tumblers felt as much a treat as it would have to his idols. To spread out and recline was to be a man assigned hectares to own. With aching bones and muscles soothed, his addled mind slowed its rotors until they spun no more.

Breath became deep and sugar sweet. Anxiety drained from his leathery hide. All fear and trepidation lay in bundles at the door. Relief had cast her spell.

He knew not how long he intended to stay. With no place to be and no commitments of which to speak, he truly felt a man at liberty in the world. He knew that these houses were not vacant forever, though there was nothing that hinted at imminent arrivals. If fortune was kind, the owners would be away for some time. While physically sprawled, he kept belongings at hand, prepared for flight at the drop of an Akubra. He embodied the dichotomy of a tabby cat - languid and lounging, yet spring-coiled and spry. He could sleep with neither eye ajar but with nerves on red alert, contorted by necessity into a creature of reaction. And if push came to shove, if his past came knocking, he'd plunge out the window and into waters below, breaching the surface with the pod of dolphins he now ogled, straddling a horizon drenched with ochre sunset tones. For now, he would sit and drink of the ocean's grace, waiting for his ships to come in.

To pass the time, he assessed his situation and, ever the thinker, he thought it to shreds. The setting brought clarity where all had been chaos. He knew the hounds of justice would still be on his trail. A detour here and a diversion there may well have gained him time, but it would not guarantee freedom. He expected that his crimes were a footnote to a header-less chapter, which read as a blessing in the skin of a curse; the trouble to find him could feasibly overcome a desire for wrongs to be righted. Submission is a Devil's deal, but it surely crossed his mind. He could cast this off as a terrible mistake, a desperate whim for which they might forgive him. The lessons learnt as a keen-eared youth finally supplanted by the lessons of life. It re-crossed his mind. It broiled and frothed. And yet... and yet, the flame that set this course ablaze still burnt a hole within. It wasn't just a matter of survival. It was a matter of continuing to strive, to welter in strife and finish the job (whatever that was). Consideration only girded intent.

Reflective as a looking glass in back-lit efflorescence, Luke paced from room to room within the prison of his mind. He knew his cause had shifted since its inception, that it had become self-sustaining and more than token reverence. It was no longer just about being a bushranger. It was about pride, defiance and achievement, about a story to be told. Though the world had swivelled and flipped on its axis, the yarns of his youth had lost none of their draw. He could never return this land to colonial times. What he could do, however, was to promulgate his own legend. His actions to date had been groundwork and training, he decided, and no shameful insignificance could tarnish future lustre. That he still roamed unimpeded was a triumph none too minor; brevity may be the soul of wit, but it is also the scourge of a saga.

Then, from the great blue yonder, he thought, for the first time in ages, of his parents; those faithful inheritors of his wrought creation, blameless except for the life they gave birth. He thought of the angst they must feel at his deeds, their noble sensibilities shuddering at the core. He was his own man forging his own legacy, yet in this moment of candour he knew it must affect others. Remote as he was, physically and emotionally, these were the people closest to him. Whatever their faults, they'd never stopped caring. They'd been nothing less than supportive. This burning compulsion was not of their making, through either rebellion or mistreated youth. To see his image on a wanted poster, to hear his name in reviling tones, to be left in the dark as searchlights probed... He knew they'd be at a loss and he tried to make it cut deep within, to feel a stabbing pain in his bones that would guide future actions. Yet that loss cut deeper, as he saw it now, because he was no longer one they could call their own. He couldn't return–not now. He had severed those bonds when he boarded the train. It was up to them to relinquish a son they could no longer know.

He poured a mug of silty coffee and let it scald his throat. It felt like days since he'd properly spoken, and he sang just to check he still could. It was croaky at first, as chords unravelled, before melting like a lozenge in the brackish coastal air. Encouraged, he launched, in muted tones, a soulful acclamation:

Bold Ben Hall, who were you when
The Darkie and his band of men
Stuck 'em up Eugowra way
With a stash of loot and demands to pay?
Was there ever evil in your bones, or were you turned to stone?
Could a loyal heart have stopped the rage 'fore it could ever start?
And they gave you the blame, might as well have the game
Oh Ben Hall, you were brave, Ben Hall, to your grave
Were you wronged and dispossessed
And driven to a viper's nest?
High up in the Weddin Hills
With a cash of loot and a bushie's skills
Was it always justice on your mind, or were your eyes turned blind?
Was the spur of infamy a spell that broke monotony?
Oh, they gave you the blame, might as well have the game
Oh Ben Hall you were brave, Ben Hall, to your grave
Bold Ben Hall, could any pact
Survive the dreaded Felons' Act?
Traitors swarming on the plain
In the ears of traps and the thrall of gain
When you felt the icy grip of treachery did conscience slip?
Purified by lead at least they took you not alive but dead

Oh, they gave you the blame, might as well have the game
Oh Ben Hall you were brave; Ben Hall: rest well in your grave

The last note resounded in shimmering vibrato, as Luke lowered his gaze and reflected that his hero may not rest as comfortably as the closing words intoned. *A mon grand regret.*

He thought some more, feet back on the table, his mind conspiring upheavals to come. He watched surging breakers defract on jagged rocks, envisioning his fragile, pinioned body dashed against the stone like kiln-fired clay. For distraction, he polished his pistols until genies came forth to hearken three wishes all one and the same. Hesitant to step outside, yet unable to sit still for long, he set about ordering all aspects of his being. Clothing was hand washed in a hasty manner, then draped over chair-backs to dry like old meat. He shaved and showered, before trimming nails and tawny locks that now flowed to his collar and beyond. Bags were unpacked, repacked and reconfigured; in the quest to draw order from chaos, every ion has its place. At the end of it all he had seen out a day, cloistered, unruffled and more or less, at peace.

His dreams that night were shards of horror, phantasmagoria from the mists of Styx. Forms shape-shifted grotesquely, with hallucinogenic intensity. One moment he sat astride a mammoth conch bursting from a burgundy sea, pursued by a trident-wielding, vengeful god, perceptibly gaining ground; the next he was trapped in a house ablaze, beams crashing with lethal force and guarding a way to various exits all locked and barred and paralysing to touch. The ultimate indignity, the oneiric *coup de grâce*, saw him alone in a field digging six feet of earth, only to disinter a one-armed girl with a revolver locked on his forehead. As the hammer cocked and she steadied the barrel, the sound of her voice brought an end to his sleep.

'This one's for you, you big fucking loser.'

He jolted upright in a whorl of confusion. He'd always been a vivid dreamer, but this was something else. His mind may have been dazed by sleep, but none of this made sense. He threw aside the sheets and stumbled out into pre-dawn gloom, banging his knee on a protruding corner and wincing in escalating pain. He cursed like a sailor and grabbed at his leg, thinking by touch he could heal it. By the time the lounge was close at hand he was spent and almost done with living. He threw down his pillow and face-planted into oblivion.

In the subsequent hours Luke finally found rest, yet the night's disruption left his plans in limbo. He had considered leaving today and meandering back to the west. Instead, when he rose mid-morning, he renewed his vows to the ocean spray. Windows open, he inhaled the bouquet of that turbulent broth. If the urge took him and nerves uncoiled, he could leave after dusk for the solace of shadows. It had served him well before. The ferocity of those nightmares had thrown him out of kilter; they were his subconscious at play, but he could do without the assault of inner virulence when he already faced threats from without. He wondered if this was a symptom of turning towards a violent, hunted lifestyle? Perhaps his mind was flinching at the man he saw himself becoming? This may have been true, but the odd, disrupted sleep was hardly enough to make him pack it in. He'd slept worse on the roots of a tree, with never a dream to speak of.

Luxuriating in the wash of high noon's light through fingerprint-smudged glass, the hoodlum appeared a man of culture, studying philosophy from a dog-eared tome. He'd found it on a shelf in this variegated home: a collection of Spinoza's thoughts, he'd chosen it for the name. The pages flicked, and his mind ticked over, challenged but never conquered. A streak of conceit made him cold to the thoughts of others, regarding his own thoughts as superior in their craft. Words piqued his interest and fluttered inside, but never left more than a momentary impression. They confirmed him, rather than changing him, because he never opened himself to their meaning. His heart was ash for the want of fire.

He was about to rise and make lunch when he heard a noise. It was unmistakable-the scratching of metal in a keyhole. He froze. Figures were silhouetted through the frosted glass door. He scurried to the bedroom and the aegis of latent weapons. He remained there in silence, senses like bottle tops ready to pop. The front door creaked open and he heard voices, resonant in increasing bewilderment.

'Hey, it looks like there's someone here.'

'I told you there was something weird about the car parked at the front.'

'Maybe they've double booked us? You have the number for the bloke we booked with?'

'Yep. Should have it on the email they sent to confirm.'

'Just what we needed after a long drive. I hope they haven't fucked up and we have to go somewhere else.'

'Here, found the number. I'll give 'em a call to see what they have to say.'

As her partner called the agent, a wary yet inquisitive young lady inspected her surroundings, from the contents of the fridge, to the map laid out on the coffee table. And she admired the view, all sea-brine and tumult.

'What did he say?'

'Definitely no double booking, from what he can tell. Seemed a bit put out that we even suggested it.'

'Well, either someone's here, or the last person left half their shit behind.'

'I know.'

'So, what do we do?'

'I guess we gather all this other person's stuff and put it outside. We've come this far, it would be a shame to just turn around and leave.'

'And what if they're here or they come back? I wouldn't feel safe staying.'

'Well, I don't want to book somewhere else unless we get our money back on this place. And old mate on the phone didn't seem too keen on a discount.'

'If you stay here, you're on your own.'

'Oh, for fuck's sake, you're such a drama queen.'

'Me? At least I'm not a tight-arse like you.'

'People, people,' came a conciliatory voice from obscurity, 'there's no need to bicker. This place is more than big enough for the three of us.'

'What the fuck?' came the response, almost in unison.

As the speaker came into view, so too did trusty metal sidekicks. At the sight of these the woman screamed, and her partner recoiled in fright. The face before them was a quandary: calm, considerate and sporting a mordant, rictus grin.

'I have to say, it's a real treat—and a bit unexpected—to have company. Such a relaxing place here, isn't it?'

'What do you want? And what are you doing here?'

'I'm on vacation, just like you. Just a happy coincidence we chose the same place.'

'You can have this place: we'll go now and leave you in peace.'

'Ha, you and I both know that wouldn't happen. You'd be straight out that door and on your way to the nearest cop shop.'

'No,', he continued, 'it's rotten luck for you, but where I go, you go.'

'Please, we have no beef with you. Just leave us alone and we'll leave you alone, promise.'

'I'm sorry. I just can't take that risk.'

'Please!'

When nouns, verbs and adjectives falter, physical force steps in. As the underdressed bushman, almost naked without his hat and boots, reached behind him for a length of cord with which to bind, he lowered one persuader and left the other fixed in sight. Sensing his moment and dosed on courage, the other man charged at his erstwhile interlocutor. Time came to a halt. Progress was glacial. Fear met fire. Then a body lay crumpled, and gouts became gushes, and the howls of a banshee permeated the air. Howls melded with weeping and life torn asunder, wailing damnation at a foe barely known. She cradled her dying lover's lolling, pallid head, as couturiers took measurements for flowing widow's weeds. Her body unable to phrase the right emotion, she pleaded for life while she bawled over death. All she was met with was coldness and dark, spreading, unending, irredeemably bleak. Screams came to a halt. The man she had hoped to marry now by funeral she'd enjoin. The culprit stood impassive. In these cruel frontier territories, no witness can be allowed to live.

- CHAPTER 14 -

Side-tracked by bullet-holes in his constitution, Owens momentarily left subordinates to hold aloft the torch. He knew it was in safe hands. That didn't stop him hankering for a return, but it allowed his head to clear somewhat. He still couldn't believe what had happened. How had he lost his mind so absurdly, so absolutely, that a rush to hug his kids had morphed into the embrace of a beer-steeped bar? Was he the man he held himself to be, or had he lived a lie that inflated with time? It fell short of being the end of the world, but he knew there was something awry, some disconnect that wrenched him from his stated path and into the arms of vice. It would be easy to cast this off as a side-effect of a confounding case, yet it felt like something more, something deeper, less benign. To discount this as stress would be too simple by half. Instead, he scraped the lining of his soul and extracted a thick, choleric paste. This was the nub of discontent. He had permitted it to build like tartar on molars: untended, unseen and malign. The cure, as he saw it, was spiritual guidance, suppressing the demon that had led him astray. The doors of his church swung wide and inviting, it watched as he stepped towards a dusty pew. It saw him take a seat and bring his head to heavy hands. He closed his eyes in prayer until they stung and almost wept. And then, in penitent reflection, he sought his wife's forgiveness and spoke to his children as he'd planned all along.

Shame drifted out and resolve swept in. Other cases had arisen, yet only one held his attention. There had been a development: the most recent means of transport in the outskirts of Omeo. He consulted a map to check where that was. When he saw that it was below the border, he hoped like hell those southern coppers wouldn't make the arrest. The car bore no badges, but it was drenched in convict DNA. This man was navigating an intrepid course, and for what purpose, apart from evading capture? Or was that indeed the sole design? It was amazing the police were reliably a step or more behind. Perhaps things hadn't changed so much in a century and a half.

Where one trail ends another must start, especially for minds with metaphysical leanings. When an Omeo doorknock found one missing wagon, the name of the culprit was fair to surmise. With limited tendrils to find and to follow, they dispatched a crew in every direction. Their roads would converge with the globe's girth transcended, and still they would be searching. In a world of constricting virtues, patience will always find room to respire. It was being tested by the lack of empirical progress and the mystifying paucity of camera footage, but it clung on fast. This man never seemed more than a frame away from their sights, more than a footstep over the horizon.

Phone calls zig-zagged the nation's south-east, eliciting updates and sharing frustration. While felonies remained in check, tensions simmered as the threat still lurked. The press kept a distance, attention diverted, yet ready to strike with a death adder's snipe. Parliamentarians bickered and quibbled, apportioning blame as if it were alms for the homeless with the polls swinging wide, like saloon doors in the breeze. The feet at whom fault lay kept shifting. And the dance those feet led could spin macabre mid-arrangement.

Owens knew implicitly that it was a matter of 'when', not 'if'. Little went unsolved these days and even less when evidence ran so deep. Confidence made fools of many and heroes of all, yet it also spurred men where others would turn on their heels. It helped Owens pick moments of action. Driven by bloody-mindedness more than prescience, both coloured his approach. For all the hard yakka to be done, it was vital to be present when the whips were cracking and the darbies clicked. He cherished the rush of an arrest well-made, the evanescence of gradually accumulated strain and the cinder-glow of completion. After years of service, it kept him feeling somewhat fresh.

Owens peered from his desk to the dutiful team, heads down like worshippers, flipping pebbles in search of an elusive fossil. They revelled in camaraderie. One would check on the injured girl; another would flesh out a case for each misdemeanour; another would study routes known and those supposed, fanning out like spokes on a wonky wheel. From grave desecration to attempted murder, every charge needed to be built from the foundations. If one piece of evidence might supplant another, there was a need to explore it, to file it in place. These were the production line workers of justice, packing and sorting until their brains screamed from overuse.

On days like this, it simply felt like a job. No more and no less. Suspense, brooding and baleful, like the lull before a raucous storm, floated thick on stuffy office air. Yet it could neither solve a case nor curse it. Achievements were measured in increments, yet in the minutiae of existence they all played a part. The same went for the world beyond these partitions, down cul-de-sacs and battle-axe blocks where coddled babes and nameless waifs all grew with every moment. The spell of civilisation was a complex, twisted magic. Owens assumed it always had been and suspected it always would be, yet surely it was never more so than now, when we'd infused such a complication. We'd trace our life's journey, or one most desired, and mirror that path in pursuit of every goal. To merely survive was no longer enough. In truth, it had long been taken for granted. In its stead, we'd shoe-horned tasks of our own creation, acts of grandeur on a plinth of sand. At least the assessment of right and wrong still revolved on a critical axis.

Behind a stockade of billowing clouds, the sun and the moon traded places for a pittance. Another day had done its dash, been run and won, given as good as it got. As disparate souls filed out into twilight, the pitter patter of accomplishment resounded on a quivering breeze.

In formative stages of the afternoon following, the landscape changed completely.

- CHAPTER 15 -

There went the Rubicon, now a rivulet fading behind. The bridge that spanned it lay scattered in rubble, clotting and damming a once peerless flow. Sirens bellowed incessant. Thoughts – what were thoughts when pure instinct took hold? Chaos enthroned passed supplication by decree. Mayhem swung cudgels with pendulous menace. All senses were haywire, competing and clamorous. Reality lagged, swirling, teasing then distant, never more than a hand-span away yet untouched. Fragmented focus pressed up against the carnage, seeking a weak point to puncture and tear. And through it all, like a dogcart-borne deity, an iron-visaged driver fought the elements for fate.

Flight had been frantic. It seemed a blur now and felt a blur then, as impulse and urgency dovetailed to action. Smoke had not yet drifted to the ground when he'd scooped up belongings and rushed for the door. It crossed his mind to rummage for money, but time, of the essence, had other ideas. The spatter of gore vaguely freckled his skin and mottled his garments. He'd expected human blood to be like any other animal's, but even in this tumult it felt like something more. As though a soul's distillation had injected each drop. He wished for a bath and a change of clothes but knew he could be long in waiting. Instead, he swore to glance elsewhere as much as he could.

He reached the precipice, breathing like a chainsaw and perspiring with porcine force. There were no backward glances. He fumbled the handle and yanked the door to the brink of its arc, then bustled through in a jumble of blunt force and torsion. For a moment he forgot which car he was driving, then, to an unseen backdrop of oscillating whitecaps, cognisance flickered and guided him forth. Hot-wired and heaving, wheels of escape soon left the seaside behind.

Expelled like a culprit of traitorous dealings, guilt was his burden but also his path. As synapses settled and awareness kicked in, the right or wrong of the situation mattered not. It was all about staying alive. For as long as he carried a soul fit to forfeit, he'd scrap tooth and claw with all foes in his way. Driving wide-eyed and blind, townscapes subsided, and he whizzed through wire-framed swards like a colonising horde. Designated speed limits increased, but it's hard to exceed full throttle. The rhythm of the car's journey rocked him out of purgatory and into the roll of new life. Progress eased to a legal clip. He finally pondered his destination. Then, as sights set on horizons to come, vision was deflected by commotion from behind. He saw it in his rear-view mirror and felt it in his marrow. A group of patrol cars had swept over a distant hill. If the road had been bowed, he never would have seen them. Involuntarily, his mind estimated them to be about three minutes in arrears. They may or may not have spotted him yet, but to see the fury of the chase was to know him a wanted man.

Traffic was constant. With one lane in each direction, dodging slow coaches took some skill. For a man whose driving history was coeval with his criminal one, he'd received a fast education. He zipped car to car and then, desperate and daring, overtook at breakneck speed. Once or twice he needed to wait, stewing in agitation while the farther lane cleared, checking his mirrors with anxious reflexes. He'd size up the slip lane but think the better of it, hoping to limit the attention attracted. Not that a car bullying its fellow road users could fail to be noticed for long. Sideways glances and looks of disapproval followed like lighthouse luminescence. The next time the glare of the beam swung around he'd be gone.

Braced for the onrush of lawmen from behind, it was something of a surprise that he proceeded as he did. The horns of his doom rang out in mournful ululation, yet while gradually closing in they couldn't overhaul. Hoping to give them the slip, or at least reduce obstacles, he turned at high velocity down a thoroughfare unknown. Usually meticulous, the haste of this mission had left him ill prepared. Devoid of local knowledge and deprived of time to study, he was running blind against an all-seeing enemy. It was only instinct guiding him now; each intersection was a gamble, with a dead end holding very clear and literal meaning. He could see a car behind him and to outrun seemed almost hopeless. He was wrestling his own four wheels, pushing boundaries he never knew to have been drawn, hanging onto the slippery outer edges of control. To stop seemed pointless. As long as the road ahead was riddled with wormholes, he'd lock them to his vision and strive with all his might.

Like a mouse in a cane-field with a snake in pursuit, he weaved here and there on a charge for his life. Right-angled rubber-scars singed in his wake and each curtain of dust drew down like it might be his last. He was shaken like a rattle wielded by a toddler with a vicious streak. He was a crash test dummy waiting for impact. And then: nothing. Through the pandemonium, he became aware of a startling absence. It was enough to distract and nearly saw him lose all control. If he had, caught in a deathroll with tonnes of sharp metal, there would have been no witness. The sirens had ceased. The chase may be better than the catch, but these hunters would never know. Needles of heart rate and speedometer dropped in solidarity. Facial muscles released their steel-trap grip. Lungs opened portals to waves of fresh respiration, tickling his throat as they shot to his brain. 'Beware of false dawns', he kept imploring, 'This could be part of their plan'. There was time to decelerate, but no time to stop.

Vigilant by nature and wary by design, he relished a minor triumph while still seeing it for what it was. This was merely the touch of swords, a welcome to the fray.

Some would say that to know the law is to fear the law. Yet when chosen paths, by design, follow neither right nor wrong, the greater fear is a failure to fulfil destiny, to fall short of lofty ambition. In bolder accomplishment something had changed, as though extremity of action itself bore rewards. Where the brush of death's whiskers had cut like a sabre, the sting of its kiss was uplifting, edifying–celestial appeasement of uppermost dread. It injected a power primeval and raw. It sheared away caution and barbs of compunction. Where a close call was a shock to the system, the act complete was a visceral thrust. He towered now, a man of uncommon substance. Notoriety was a fleeting price to pay. In the aftermath of his fulmination, there seemed to be no stain that could not be scrubbed away.

The late afternoon bequeathed radiance to these season-ravaged ranges and brought a bold proliferation from burrows, nests and holes. These denizens of frost and fire knew well the times of want. Within their bones they understood the paradox of nature's wrath. They knew their place and accepted it for what it was: opportunity, not restriction. They crooked their necks as a reaper of whirlwind sought sanctuary in their subsistence. And they shook their heads as, mired in fixation, the newcomer flattered this domain with inflated majesty. Then, curiosity gone, they turned away and sniffed out their next morsel. Let this beast ride in on wisps of delusion. It was, after all, no fault of his that as a mother's son, placenta-born and clumsily bipedal, he could not see the wood for the trees.

- CHAPTER 16 -

The collective jaw of a country dropped. An innocent couple, lives and dreams incipient and boundless, mowed down in cold blood. Such things were just not meant to happen, not in this land and not in these enlightened times. Had it happened overseas, it would have affirmed the local way. Instead, inverse, and perverted, it was an anomalous affront to freedoms hard-won. A nation beyond reproach will always find excuses. Meanwhile, those at the coalface were more concerned with finding the culprit.

Good news may travel fast, but bad news loses little in comparison. Alerted to a fleeing set of spinning wheels, highway cruisers set their sights and homed in on the target. The resultant chase was a cut and thrust death-race, truncated when those behind realised they had more for which to live. Convinced they'd been on the heels of a maniac, it was enough to jot down details and then fight another day. As dust clouds like snowflakes floated to the duco of stationary cars, time caught up and escorted them back to base. There, mildly chastened, they licked their grazes with a mother cat's tenderness, while shaking their heads at a lunatic's reckless abandon.

Damned by their duty, South Coast police made the first gruesome incursions, following up a neighbourly call of alarm. Recoiling in sickened horror, and ensuring the coast was clear (or the Coast was clear, as their job entailed), the fall-guys of discovery called for backup and reverted to process. Their latex-gloved hands explored and examined. Haunted vision pleaded for compartmentalisation. Camera lenses squinted to restrict the trauma. Minds reeling found strength in new calling; the shock of the scene was a spur to bring justice, to honour the grief of those soon to be told. They were barely even aware of the crashing edifice behind, a sempiternal swell that could not wash the crimson tide.

They found a range of effects at the property. Some belonged to the deceased, but others, such as assorted cans of non-perishables, hair-bedraggled toiletries, and unemptied rubbish bins, pointed to another occupant, to the proverbial snake in the grass. Calls to the owner confirmed as much: the property should have been vacant for close to a fortnight (bleeding money, but now's no time to whinge— others have bled more and for less) before the couple's tragic arrival. Cleaners swore blind they'd left the place spotless. When tenants nearby confirmed seeing a stranger at the house in recent days (though thinking nothing of it, as this was almost commonplace) the picture became clearer. When they gave a rough description, the police were left with little doubt. Whatever his purpose, the attacker had been waiting. Whatever the intent, two corpses bore his name. Whatever it took, and wherever it took them, there were pullulating masses determined to track him down.

Hearts in the Central West sank like stones. A pall of recognition descended long before any official announcement. The deed marked a sanguinary escalation, and they all knew whose blood daubed thick on those hands. Where guilt had no place, it burrowed like weevils, boring holes of doubt in procedure's rigid form. Over and over self-recrimination cycled, as downcast cops picked on angles cast over, delving where diligence had taken them before. They felt the agony of death's cruel admittance: unbidden, unwelcomed and deceitfully unkind. The po-faced Senior Sergeant felt the same pain and emptiness; he felt it slightly less than his colleagues, but it still rattled him to the core. In practised reverence, he muttered a quiet prayer that like a stringent tincture re-energised his being. In devastation, they might still find strength.

Phones rang like church bells at midday, while emails pinballed back and forth, side to side, up and down. Somewhere in this imbroglio there'd be a glimpse of reason, a guiding light and course to pursue, but they needed to find it. They needed to find *him*. No more beating around the bush (though beating *within* the bush would be both permissible and expected) and no more reactionary policing. They had to drill into this increasingly misanthropic brain, decipher motives and foretell what might unfold. One thing seemed beyond question: having outlasted the chase, the newly minted killer was bound to take stock in nature's arbour. That just seemed to be what he did. And given where he'd come from and the heat now singeing his tail, chances were that he wasn't far removed. It led to thinking, how was it that in a land of such vast deforestation a man could still find wooded swathes in which to vanish? The answer was one no servant in blue could bear to consider.

By virtue of familiarity, Owens and his team were taken into the confidence of inquiries far away. The groundwork done, and knowledge gained, were tender of immeasurable value. While a Sydneysider, born and bred, and late of the Sapphire Coast, it was on the Central plains that this demoniac spectre formed. Those were their wells he'd drunk from, their waters he'd sullied. He'd polluted their legends, run roughshod through their history and disrupted present-day lives. For a man who'd sworn to do quite the opposite, it was a significant achievement. Sometimes, Owens felt, in the strength of our delusions we can transplant the sun for the moon. At other times, we convince ourselves that both are illusory tools of diversion. What should be undeniable loses traction in the mud of twisted minds. This outlaw could sketch reality to suit his own image—all colonial hues, European ignorance and spear-carrying savages—yet he could never avoid being a part of another, greater picture. And with each callous, self-serving outrage, his own reality held less and less importance.

The day wound down like a tired spinning top, turning in diminishing circles, then falling flat with a sinistral whimper. Emotionally drained and yearning for support at close quarters, officers ghosted away to their homes. For Owens, this would presage a journey south-east, where he had been invited to join the ancillary hunt. It was better than nothing, but so was swallowing razor blades. Not that he had a lot of say in the matter. Nor did his wife when the news was conveyed before dinner that night.

'How long do you think you'll be?', she asked, mildly querulous.

'Depends on how things pan out. How long's a piece of string, I guess. I'll be in touch though.'

'Of course. Sorry, it's your job and I know it's important.'

'By the way', she continued, 'Eliza got suspended from school today.'

'Oh, what for?'

'Fighting. Apparently, another girl picked on her and she settled it with her fists.'

'Eliza? Really? That doesn't sound like her at all.'

'I guess kids change a lot when you don't pay attention.'

'What's that supposed to mean?'

'How much do you know about what our kids are up to? When did you last take the time to talk to them?

'When did they last show an interest in talking to us?'

'They're kids, Steve. We're adults. We're the ones who need to take the high ground here, to make an extra effort. If we don't, we risk losing them forever. You realise that?'

'Sure, but what do you want me to do? I can't force them to open up.'

'No, but you can give them the opportunity. Lend a supportive ear. Ask what they're doing. I know work's busy and I know there's a lot on your mind, but this is more important than anything right now.'

'So, you'd rather I dropped out of this case, or took a back seat?'

'No, no, not at all. But could you maybe use the time you have better, to connect with the kids before it's too late?'

'And with you?'

'I could always use more time with you, but it's the kids who really need you right now.'

'I know, but I guarantee they'd rather play with their phones or computers than talk to me.'

'That might be true, but with a bit of perseverance and patience–two things I know you're really good at–it will work wonders.'

'How long's Eliza suspended for?'

'How about you ask her?'

With a shrug of the shoulders and a sigh from the depths of his diaphragm, Owens rose from the couch and moved, lumbering, towards a chamber of teenage maelstrom.

'Steve,' came a voice from behind, almost ethereal, 'You're a good man. I love you.'

Having paused at the sound, he continued in silence.

It took three raps for the door to be opened, for the hum of music to ascend to a roar. The face before Owens was aloof yet defiant, eyes meeting his with steely inscrutability.

'Hey sweetie, can I come in?'

A shrug of the shoulders was followed by retreat into the room. Owens followed; senses dazzled by the rush of teenage paraphernalia. He didn't remember so many posters on those subtle pastel walls. He wasn't offered a seat, but he took one all the same, and asked for the music to be turned down.

'Your mum told me what happened at school today.'

'Yeah? What did she say?'

'Just that you got in a fight with a girl who was picking on you.'

'Well, she was. And she got what she deserved.'

'That's no way to speak, Liza.'

'But it's true.'

'You remember what we taught you about turning the other cheek?'

'Yeah, but–'

'–but nothing. As tempting as it might seem, you can't fix these things with violence. That makes you no better than the girl who was picking on you.'

'Whatever.'

'How long are you suspended for?'

'Just a day.'

Owens gathered his thoughts.

'I'm disappointed in you, sweetie, but we can't undo what's been done. Can you promise me you'll try to learn from this and maybe act differently in the future?'

'Yeah, I suppose so. I got her good, though.'

'I'm sure you did. Just next time, maybe try words instead.'

The next morning, packed and prepared, he ate breakfast while reading the usual alarmist broadsheet. The leading story was all too familiar: it had bled through his dreams and punctuated sleep. His wife was making lunches and juggling conflictions of health and nutrition. One kid emerged and shuffled, disaffected, while the others, vampiric, clung to dark with mortal fright. How could his words bring them back to the straight and narrow? It was all he could do to lead by example, give them their space, and assist and console when requested. They weren't bad kids, really. And he should know. He'd dealt with a few.

Breakfast passed with minimal conversation. Within these confines, what was there to talk about anyway? If he'd gritted his teeth any more, he'd soon chew his bacon and eggs with slivers of enamel. As soon as he was out the door, with a lingering kiss of disconnection, he lunged for his phone and dialled the first colleague he could think of. The conversation that ensued was ardent and enthused. It filled him with rapture as the weight of restraint drained free of his body. It sharpened his mind and stroked his sense of purpose. When key found ignition and foot met floor, he was already in another place.

Mid-afternoon shadows blanketed the dairy-rich plains at the hoof of the state. Devouring the source of that opaline richness, a mix of pied blotches and raven-black hides shone with diamantine luminance. The first thing to strike Owens on arrival was how gently the claws of winter had caressed these parts. That was worth a photo or two for posterity. The second thing to strike him was how organised and efficient the local force appeared to be. Some prejudices exist for the sole purpose of being refuted. Owens met with the local top brass and was brought up to speed on latest developments, of which there were more than a few. He smiled upon hearing that none involved capture or conviction. They did, however, open the curtain to an all too real stage-show of horror, with the central actor their leading man. Whatever doubt remained fritted away, as evidence mounted like a pile of skulls.

The area commander, a no-nonsense character and a bulwark of a woman, pulled Owens aside for further consultation.

'That bastard made a real mess of those kids.'

'Yeah, so I hear.'

'I don't care how many resources it takes; I'm not sleeping until that arsehole is behind bars.'

'Of course. I'm with you all the way.'

'Now, you've dealt with this scumbag a bit. What do you know about him?'

'I'm not entirely sure. I mean, he keeps surprising me, keeps coming up with a new crime to commit.'

'Sure, but he's not committing tax evasion. He's a violent bugger, isn't he?'

'Yes and no. I think he is becoming more violent as he becomes more desperate and more entrenched in this lifestyle.'

'Lifestyle? You talk about it like it's a choice, like becoming a surfer or something.'

'I'm very much of the belief that we all choose our paths in life. We all have good and evil inside and it's up to us to choose which we follow. Some of us have a leaning to one or another, often because of our upbringing. But in his case, it seems he's carved out a niche when he absolutely didn't need to.'

'So, you think he's almost doing this for fun? To get some kind of perverted kicks?'

'Not quite, I haven't quite got a handle on that. But he's playing out a role with deadly consequences for those he meets.'

'Not bloody wrong there.'

'I met his parents. Spoken to them on numerous occasions. A nicer, more helpful couple you couldn't hope to meet. I've spoken to co-workers, to –'

'–Co-workers? He's not working alone?'

'Sorry, co-workers from previous jobs. And friends, not that he's had much to do with them for some time. I haven't found a single bad egg among them.'

'What about this bushranging malarkey? Do you think there's anything to that, or just a beat-up?'

'I think there's definitely something to it. For whatever reason, I think he's living out a delusion that he's Ned Kelly or something, that he can be an old-time bushranger in a modern world.'

'Christ.'

'He's marginalised himself, and now he's trying to get by in that narrow corridor of existence. It's this that's made him dangerous.'

'And now that he's killed, assuming he hasn't before—'

'—Which we don't think he has—'

'—there's nothing holding him back. He's crossed that last line.'

'Yep, he's left any good behind and truly thrown his hat in with evil.'

'Fucken hell. There's a lot of grieving people out there just because of one bloke's hobby.'

'I know. Sometimes a man doesn't know just what he's capable of until he sees how it affects others.'

'Crikey, you bring any more philosophy to this town and they'll put you in the loony bin.'

'I'm worried that's where they'll put him, assuming we take him alive.'

'But surely he's as sane as piece of sandpaper? He knows what he's doing.'

'I agree. I've just lost my faith in the courts a bit these days.'

'Well, if we take him alive, we'll find out, I guess. You up for a mission tomorrow?'

'Absolutely. Not here for a picnic.'

'We've been scouring the local area and the bush in particular, based on what we understand about his habits. There's a tranche of land up here', with which she pointed to a green smudge on an unfolded map, 'and there's some suggestion his car was seen in the vicinity not long after the aborted chase.'

'Sounds a good place to start.'

'We checked other areas overnight with no joy. I was ready to sink the slipper into you for not finding this ratbag, but it seems he is a bitch to catch.'

'He is. I've questioned myself and my team over this, but yep, he's slippery. He blends well into his surroundings and knows how to live off the land.'

'Yet there's one of him and fuck knows how many of us. Thanks for the chat, Steve. I've got an appointment with the media that I'd love to get out of, but you know what they're like.'

He nodded and shaped a grin that was almost a grimace. Then he was alone in a crowd of officers, information dispersing left, right and centre. The Great Divide rose Himalayan in magnitude. It could prop up the Heaviside Layer for all he cared. White man may have strained to cross it two hundred years before, but Owens couldn't see the fuss.

At his digs for the evening, the infrequent traveller was, at first, a fish out of water. Then, boots off and feet up, he allowed the tranquillity to consume him. Waiting for the kettle to sputter and boil, he placed a call home and found consolation there. Nothing seemed so bad from a distance. Any knot run gnarled and tangled could be undone with perspective and time. He crossed the room to the bar fridge, seeking milk for his coffee and opening a lolly shop of liquid temptation. He pulled out a bottle and spun it in his hand. No one would ever know. He took in the logo, the lurid badge of submission. Memories swept through him like hot and cold flushes. When he walked away, bottle-tops untwisted sat like caps of soldiers on parade, all present and correct. And his milk-infused coffee steamed like geysers from sanctified earth.

Along his journey south, in a sun-bleached village of fallowed inheritance where they'd stopped for a bite to eat, he'd happened on a second-hand bookstore of dust-bound antiquity. Perusing the shelves with customary attention to detail, his eyes stalled on one of Frank Clunes' old potboilers. The condition was decent and the price loose change. Before he knew it, he was peeling the sticker from the cover and stowing the purchase in his suitcase. Now, senses pinged by caffeine, he delved into the annals of a history back in vogue. It was more a case of flicking through than assaying cover to cover. He found the lead characters craven and uncouth: far from the exemplifiers of liberty they'd been painted. No one leapt from the page to shout: 'Follow me!'. He appreciated it was another time and that life in those days bred folk that were tough and unpredictable. He felt a modicum of sympathy for simple souls in fear for their lives and under the spell of derring-do. Yet a sinner is a sinner, and a reprobate is never more or less than his actions. That such men were idolised he could never understand. These were bad men, misdemeanants, drunkards to be cursed with spiritual poison. More to the point, in a land of war heroes, explorers, philanthropists, inventors, statesmen, dignified athletes and artistic types, surely there were more worthy people to extol? As patience wore thin and the drug released its hold, he fell fast asleep, no closer to comprehension.

To Luke, it was as clear as day, and this day shone with almost diaphanous clarity. He'd gone to sleep a bushranger and he sure as hell woke as one, replete with stiff back from a bed of twigs and tenterhooks. What rest he succumbed to was riven, at regular intervals, by a noise in the darkness, a signal for a coming showdown. The bush was a sentinel jumping at shadows. Somewhere in the depths of that crepuscule, all-knowing and ill-tempered, his fouled and harrowed conscience cackled like a witch. The natural world wasn't so friendly now, but north of the abyss, it was the only world he had.

Without a map to refer to, wits were now his sole and trusted guide. He didn't know quite where he was, though he guessed it was one of the vast stretches of eucalypt reservation swollen like fat along the tendon of the Far South Coast. It crossed his mind that somewhere to the north, not so far on corvine wings, the Clarkes and Connells had in blood parlayed. Dumping his car down a rough-hewn fire trail, he'd continued by foot, first with solar impetus, then under torch-lit auspices. He'd groped and scrapped through land not fit for men, in the hope that where he strove, by necessity, others would surrender. Progress was sluggish, but with no way of knowing precisely what time was in hand, he'd just kept going. When the light went out and the scrapping ceased, an igneous wedge conferred shelter on a shivering fugitive.

As he warmed his hands over a timid fire—a risk worth dying for; a heat worth burning for—his ossified sight stripped the bark of trees to flay. He noticed the sap-stains and scribbles of larvae, the knobbly junction of branches and trunk, grey-grown foliage both shield and sword, canopy dwellers all action and life. Their secrets unravelled after careful perquisition. They'd seen his heroes, or men in their image. Their branches had been used to build their shanties, their shacks and their lean-tos; they'd supported the desperate while they hung from the noose. They'd flinched at genocide's chilling calculation; they'd taunted the flagellant while bound to his captive and, punishment done, they watched over graves. The world, so changed, in constancy moved forward. Whatever his sins, these giants had seen worse. In the delusion of early light, that was tacit approval.

Plump droplets of rain splashed into his morning cuppa. That was breakfast, beginning and end. With the bulk of supplies sealed in evidence bags, the bite of privation was now taking hold. He doused the fire and melded the ash with twigs and leaves, then rolled his swag and descended the ledge. It wasn't obscure enough to serve as a retreat, nor enclosed enough to act as a fort, yet he would remember it, even as he did all he could to ensure it would never remember him. He set off through territory dense and demanding, trusting deliverance to be more than a trap. He may be running from a world he'd eventually need to face, but now was no time to confront it. Monastic and resourceful, he could forage an existence until his image had faded from view. For all the inanities of modern existence, its dwindling attention span might pave the way to redemption.

More bulldozing wombat than forest sprite, he gradually moved deeper into the bushland. Once or twice he took a tumble and cursed the fate that had led him here. He watched a falcon hover above, transfixed by its effortless arc of predation. He drank in the ashen eyes of a petrified deer and thought of his belly only after she'd bolted. The nature around was so keen and so vital that he hardly thought about what he had done. What he was doing stretched the limits of focus—elasticised as those boundaries might be. And if it was merely delaying the inevitable, well, that was now every purpose he served. To avoid going arse over head was of primary concern. The secondary concern gave birth to the first: fresh water was needed, and that required descent.

Down through the bracken he made his measured way. Saplings snapped and folded back like callipers bent to extend. He skated over lichened rocks or skirted close beside them, grabbing whatever appeared secure to ease the risk of peril. In many places, footholds were only the sludge of leaves gone rotten. A centipede crept from this morass to his hand, but it failed to draw a reaction. Nor did the orb weaver dropping from high like a free faller bound for his cheek. Flies and mosquitoes were an annoyance, but other invertebrate forest-dwellers were hard pressed to make him flinch. He was a forest-dweller himself. He continued, and when he heard the chime of a bubbling flow, jangling in duet with haughty bell miners, he increased the pace, justification triumphant within. He may have learnt to take human life, but he still had the skills to preserve it.

At water's edge he set down his pack, removed his hat and cupped slightly murky liquid to his face. It streamed down hollowing cheeks and snagged in his beard, curdling in messy refreshment. He repeated the process, soaking his hair in Acherontic run-off while oars of the ferryman stroked unknowable repetitions. In these waters he sensed a nexus, though he couldn't explain why. All he knew was that layers of consternation drained from his being and ligatures of sin fell like snow to the ground. The past washed away. Cleansed, he left his pack, removed his boots, rolled up his trousers and waded upstream with flask in hand. The river ran clearer there, and he filled his mouth and canteen in quick succession. By the time he parted ways with this otherworldly flow, his belly was squelching, and his consciousness mollified.

In mid-afternoon, serenity broke, as the whir of helicopter blades yelped in the distance. Closer they came, these motorised aerial inquisitors, deafening insects that scanned the landscape below, blades beating like oversized hummingbird wings. He made himself small, taking cover under fallen boughs lain transom-like, criss-crossing the forest floor. Any glance from above must have been cursory, as no sooner had the noise reached a peak than it receded into the background, trading places with the gentle lilt of the bush. Then it circled back, almost expecting a lapse that was not forthcoming. When the coast seemed clear at last, Luke rolled out of hiding and marched on through the densest scrub on offer. It seemed they were now coming at him from every angle. He peered to the ground and dared it to do its worst. Should chthonic talons burst forth while he slept, no part of this man would have been surprised.

When he happened on a limestone cave of enticing depths and a eucalypt standing on guard, he was quick to call it his own. Not that he had competition, apart from whatever ophidian riffraff might cool their blood until springtime. He made camp and stretched his aching frame, increasingly gaunt yet wiry as a vagrant canine. The evening was cool, though rain had long ceased, leaving rock pools to dip in but not to drink. Dinner was a tin of beans that he didn't bother heating. There would be no fire tonight. Wrapped like a body in grave robbers' wake, he shivered his penitence through to the bone. By torchlight he read for as long as he could to pass the time and ward off reflection. At least he had experience of nights outdoors; before he set out on this path, he'd wondered how people used to pass the time after sunset. He figured the size of their families was a clue.

Sleep came with ease to his joint-weary form. He rested as one with the surrounding vastness, yet the vastness within would not silence for long. It chose the hour after midnight to strike and held him in torment until the onset of vermillion dawn. All he could do was lie there and suffer a mind's unbidden excoriation. It began as a nightmare, an odious vision of his childhood bedroom, door flung open and bodies strewn in terrible, familiar repose. He watched as troopers filed past and dragged each stiffening body from the point of expiration to the sombre world outside. There, they were propped on stools as shutters snapped a grizzly memento. He crept towards the lifeless models, admiring the cut of their lower-class Victorian garb. Upon reaching them, he lifted drooping heads and stared into the emptiness of soul-abandoned sockets. As the troopers looked on in impassive supervision, the shock of agnate recognition scuttled his senses. He woke in a sweat that belied the icy climate. Like an early motion picture, the dream played out in soundless, colourless frames, yet each second was etched in his rattled consciousness. He inhaled and let the collected air whistle through pursed lips. The content of the dream seemed laced with portentous meaning, yet it was the tone that held greater concern. In the weakness of ruptured sleep, he knew he'd committed crimes at odds with all he'd been taught. With everything he knew to be right and wrong. For all his swagger and bravado, be it affected or gained, he was worlds away from the gentleman outlaw he'd set out to be. Why had this happened? How had he permitted such complete and utter deviation? In this habitat of bats and invertebrate artisans, his subconsciousness would grant no rest until it chiselled out the truth.

Thoughts by night come like brumbies from back gullies, wild and untainted by human incursion. They refuse to bow to laws of the day, of rational comprehension, of measured consideration and, most of all, of welcome distraction. Locked in a crocodilian death roll, they submerged Luke in a threshing squall of pernicious introspection. Two faces returned: death masks of his own creation. They swayed to the sound of steel rendering flesh and the release of life from florid quintessence. Repressed in the chaos of flight, these memories now returned in flood.

That poor couple: fatally in the wrong place at the worst imaginable time. Surely, he could have knocked them out, or negotiated an agreement? When he harked to the impulse to go for his guns, he knew where the kernel of doom had been sown. To set a certain tone is to narrow the point of conclusion.

The breadth of reflection swept west of the range, to the first haze of gun smoke and bawls in the night. While the thrill of notoriety had muffled those cries, they'd merely lain cold and disconsolate. Now, they traded freedom for a place in this overwhelming fug.

He was a killer, and his mind at this hour would not let him forget. Eyes closed and with hands over ears, he sought the distraction and solace of slumber. It was hopeless. Eventually, patience burnt down to the wick, he sat up and stared with possum eyes into the pitch-black infinite. He pressed the switch of his torch on and off, a nervous impulse and trick of illumination: 'By light let me see and by light leave me blinded'.

Here he was, perched on a rock in benighted isolation. Giving up on sleep at least removed one front on which to fight. It was a minor comfort. Contemplation held fast but was difficult to grasp, a blur of tangents and angles in diametric enmity. Restless as a gypsy, the saboteur within roared with recrimination. It echoed the voice of the young girl in his dreams: 'This one's for you, you big fucking loser.' As daybreak kissed the horizon, so came acceptance. He wished that much could be undone, but if time could spin backwards just where would it end? Truth be told, if it could rotate forward, he would have taken that as well. Instead, what's done is done and that to come needs shape to take effect. By the time his brain buckled and succumbed to fatigue, he was drunk on the calls of whipbirds shimmering through the trees.

- CHAPTER 17 -

The southern front mobilised like a tank division on training wheels. This was unfamiliar ground for many of those gathered, though not for Owens, who had tracked a fugitive through Blue Mountains wilderness and clamped him with handcuffs at the search's end. This memory, from what felt like a lifetime ago bobbed to the surface, providing as much in positive thought as it ever could in guidance. Let youth have its energy: experience carries its own advantage. They had deployed scouts throughout the area, with little to report except scratches and bramble-tattered uniforms, until one located a lonesome car, thrashed to within an inch of the wrecker's yard and covered with a makeshift bower. Those who'd choked on its petrol fumes needed no second description. That vehicle became a coruscating totem for the searchers and their quest. To the public, the 'beachfront abattoir' served a similar purpose. Horror and contempt held fast, producing incendiary and unflagging reports that razed innumerable sheaves of newsprint. The story read the same, no matter how it was written. The words in their sympathy flittered every way but one.

Owens felt the rush of expectation. He may have seen his role to be less than he deserved, but he would never baulk at the chance to put skills to the test and extend the long limbs of justice. Besides, the welcome mat was so graciously set by the local force that any chagrin was quickly allayed. Taken into confidences and regularly asked for input, the sound of silence was a mark of respect. Foremost in all minds was the task at hand, and if petty differences were to raise their head, they at least had the decency to keep these tensions subservient to the common cause. By noontide on the day following Owens' arrival, he was shoulder to shoulder with like-minded souls, an organism sustained by a single source, to the soundtrack of cordial banter and war stories of yore. They set out in clusters from base camp erected in rickety impermanence on patchily grassed land. They sniffed out tracks, at the whim of a broken sapling, a flaking of bark, a hint of tread in desiccant mud: anything and everything that might illumine the way. And if they found nothing, there was always that bucket of rust on which to fall back. Shapeshifter or stygian drifter, he had to be in here somewhere.

Based on the principle that no rat escapes a cage with the exits boarded up, and that a rodent denied a way out will eventually engorge its own, the squeeze was on. Pincer-like and reinforced, the gambit of the hunt was manifest. Agreed reckoning was that they were at a roughly fifty-hour disadvantage. Still, that didn't feel like a problem. Being ahead of the pack counts for little when there's nowhere left to run.

Owens cursed his rugby-playing days as he trudged into the forest. He was part of a group of ten, each laden with a pack and supplies for the unknown time ahead. They wore the insignia under which they served, though bowing to comfort over rigid formality. The troopers of old turned green in their graves, cursing the formality of their times. Contact with the outside world was constant, utilising contemporary methods to monitor progress and update whereabouts. If the voice at the other end was less than supportive, technology could reliably find mysterious ways to fail. As the party settled into something of a rhythm, it seemed a matter of time before steps were triumphantly retraced. Even those who, by experience, knew better were caught in the winds of wreathing optimism. It was ballast in the eyes of storm and motivation, thick or thin. It seemed to Owens that when it came to hope, the gulf between hunter and hunted was growing.

Every man is a searcher. It's only that some are aware of the fact and actively track their pursuit, while others meander in the blindness of distraction, focus stricken, and obstacles bloated beyond reason. Where spiritual labours enlighten some, they'll break the back of others or riddle with desolation. Sometimes the more linear the quest, the better. Abstraction eschewed bears no weight of dismay, drying its powder for times to come. To those who crack the exploratory whip, reward is a panoply of life at its richest, for to search is to court accomplishment, and accomplishment makes sovereigns of all. If only life would permit us to know it, would let the taste linger for more than a while. One ending is many thousand beginnings. The search only ends when the torch goes out forever.

Like beasts in migration they lumbered on, separating at forks in the path and reconvening with a shake of the head. Not a corner was cut. Any sign of humanity was collected and sealed. Owens would have been surprised if the tidy devil had slipped in his ways, but he'd never picked him as a murderer either. He dutifully retrieved refuse from the forest floor–chocolate wrappers, plastic bottles and even a mud-encrusted shoe–and added each piece to his collection. Two days in arrears, expectations were hazy, phantom tails flickering in the breeze. A man could walk his soles to the bone, or he could nest at first convenience. As chopper blades knifed through the sky above, Owens wondered what he'd do in such a situation. 'I'd get as far away as possible, as quickly as possible', he mumbled, 'and I'd hope that by the time they found me, the world had forgotten.' He steeled himself to remember.

'Hey, have a look at this', came a call from one of the local officers, motioning at a guttered section of track. The others gathered around.

'Looks like it might be a match. I'll take some photos, but we'll need to take a mould.'

'Thank god for the recent rains, eh?'

'Bloody oath. Hard to get a footprint in dust.'

'Nice work picking that up, Eagle Eyes.'

'Tell that to the missus. She reckons I never see what's going on.'

'Women, eh?'

'Yeah, women. Can't live with 'em, can't taser 'em.'

Owens reeled in disgust. He opened his mouth to speak but thought better of it.

The camera flashed from all angles. Cordoned off and marked, this was a fresh starting point. It also presaged the coming of darkness and the need to bivouac before chill took hold. They would rest tonight on stomachs filled with charcoaled meat and crusty bread. They would wake in the morning to chip away at the task at hand until a soul's declension was a gaol cell's encumbrance.

Out of mobile phone range, Owens missed the chance to reach out. If it bothered him, he never let on, regaling his audience with monologues of life beyond the Divide, cold truths and white lies a rat king of narration. The officers took care to keep voices low, while each took their turn to act as a sentinel. Watchers avoided red faces, yet time must pass, and in anticipatory silence stories will yearn to be told. The raconteur scanned the vitreous eyes and ruddy cheeks of his audience and felt a kinship, innate and inspiring. These bonds transcended regional lines; shared training and common purpose count for plenty in the shallows of human interaction. The Senior Sergeant's face infused with mellowing smugness as another jape hit the mark. The comforts of home could wait for a while.

'So, what drove you to become a cop, Steve?'

The question came from one of the younger officers, delivered between sips of a breakfast tonic.

'No word of a lie, I joined the force to make a difference, to help people.'

'Noble man. I like it.'

'How about you?'

'The old man was a cop. Seemed the obvious, natural thing to do. And I wasn't much chop at school, so I figured this would give me discipline and a decent career.'

'You sound pretty noble yourself.'

'You reckon you've done that?' drifted a voice from slightly further afield.

'Done what?'

'Made a difference. Helped people.'

'Yeah, I think so. I sometimes forget, lose track, get distracted, but then I think back to some cases I've been involved in–and not just the high-profile ones. People done over or down on their luck that I've given an inkling of hope to. Anyone could have done it, but I've been lucky to have the chance to help. It fills me with a sense of pride, I guess.'

'You seriously reckon anyone could do what we do?'

'I don't know. Probably not. But with the right training and experience, sure, why not? We're no different to anyone else, really.'

'I call bullshit on that.'

The gruffness of the tone was a morning jolt.

'We were born to do this job. Sure, others might have been as well and decided on something else, but you can't tell me that just anyone could lob in and do this for a living. Call it fate or whatever you like, we're fulfilling our destiny as upholders of the law.'

'Okay, fine. Then how does someone find out if they were born for it or not?'

'Well, it was obvious to us. I know we come from different backgrounds, upbringings and everything, but we figured it out. Our calling found us, and others.'

'Wasn't obvious to me,' came a voice from behind. 'Took me ages to figure out what I wanted to do.'

'Me neither,' added another.

'Okay, well maybe not obvious, but I can assure you it was in our blood somewhere.'

'And what about young men and women who join the force to right some kind of wrong, who were bullied as kids, or worse?'

'Their calling reached them in a roundabout way. Look, I'm not claiming we all got here the same way–would be boring if we did–but we are society's protectors, through and through.'

'So recruits who drop out, for whatever reason, are ones who thought they had this magical calling but were mistaken?'

'More or less. They couldn't cut it because the job's not for them. Never was, and possibly never will be.'

'That's brutal, mate.'

'Maybe, but think about it: would you want to give weapons, authority, power to someone who wasn't designed for it? It's a harsh world, and something predestined us to be its enforcers.'

'Sounds like someone's been watching too many Arnie movies.'

The debate had been congenial, but the jovial interjection was timely.

'Hey, Steve, see if you can help young Phil over there. Needs a hand to see some common sense.'

The man of the western plains smiled before responding, 'Sorry, no can do. My job is to help the unfortunate, not the intransigent.'

Owens rose and walked away.

Apertures in cloud-cover sprinkled sunlight over the searchers as they set out from their camp in the hours next to dawn. The going was easy enough, following established paths with only nugatory diversions. Senses were sharp as blackberry thorns, as keen as the rotors that continued to intermittently hum overhead. What eyes couldn't see, what ears couldn't hear, what noses couldn't smell was left to the devices of cold intuition. The park had been temporarily closed to the public, so there was limited risk of either obstruction or contamination. This domain was theirs to pick over like carrion and scorch with investigative ardour. By reducing impediments, this man had done them something of a favour. This maze of forestation may have presented challenges, but it had obviated others. And as the clock-hands ticked away, the greatest challenge of existence was the least of their concerns.

Deeper into the reserve they walked. Reports from outside did nothing but confirm identity and stay the course. Maybe it was the influence of nature on urbanised souls, but the relative isolation felt nurturing. Away from the din and redundant chatter of a restless society greasing its wheels, they were far from the questions, if not closer to answers, with fair leave taken from the temporal world. This was toil and repetition, but it was also a release. As Owens thought, whimsically, you could charge good money to be part of this.

While far from standing still, they were playing a waiting game. They didn't need a fox's stealth—at least, not yet—but they could do with her stamina. And they needed her awareness of where prey might be. They assumed the fugitive would seek shelter at dusk and water by day. They assumed he'd source whatever heat he could to keep the freezing nights at bay. They assumed he'd otherwise seek cover or camouflage to elude the spies above. He'd go as deep into the bush as possible. They assumed that when cornered he'd strike like a wharfie at Christmas. They were reasonable, salient assumptions based on years of experience. Yet for one of the party, at least, they came with a sobering caveat. This man was far from a criminal mastermind, and it was this relative naivety that made him unpredictable, that had rendered him an unknown quantity. Just as an arachnophobe's fear is based, in part, on a spider's capacity for caprice, so too did the furrows encroaching a sun-lined brow reflect concerns advanced beyond reason.

The trefoil-shaped glade at which they lunched was like a prison cell fed sunlight through plumb and ferrous bars. As muscles cooled down, so too did the weather, or so it seemed to those in its midst. Still, they'd take this over a summer hunt any day; flies, leaches, snakes and sweat quickly turn a man's eyes blind to the most frightful of transgressions. Owens was seated with spine against pack, brushing crumbs from stubbled dishevelment. His knees were aching, but he kept that to himself. His thoughts, however, were another matter.

'I know we've not been out here long, but I'm sure stinging for a hot shower', came a wistful voice from his left.

'Yeah, me too', piped the jaded voice of a senior constable.

'Could do with a proper bloody bed.'

'And a Thai massage while you're at it?'

'Only if you're the one giving it, mate. With an extra happy ending.'

'How you going over there, Steve? Missing home?'

'Not really. Probably sounds a bit silly, but this feels like home at the moment.'

'Too right it sounds silly. You've lost your marbles, mate.'

'Tell you what, Steve, we'll pay for you to get a rub and tug when we're out of this place.'

'Ha, thanks. You're too kind. You can explain it to my missus while you're at it.'

'She's probably shacked up with another bloke by now, anyway. You probably have a few other sisters you can hook up with though, don't you?'

The recipient of the jibe was an island in a sea of schoolyard humour. He knew better than to react; the faces of his kids flashed before him and something about practise and preaching came to mind.

'Seriously though, you must be hoping this is over soon and you can head back west?'

'I look forward to heading back when the job is done.'

'Mate, if you were any squarer, they'd put you in a pack of SAOs.'

'Ha-ha, I think I could live with that.'

'Just hope you don't mind having vegemite and butter squeezed through you.'

'Trust me, I have three kids. I've put up with worse.'

The search continued, with the western guest turning despondent as a petrel trapped in a tempest.

'What would you do if you had to give this game away?'

The question was from leftfield and the answer no different.

'I'd fight to get it back.'

'Sure, but what if you had no choice? If you got crook, or worse?'

'I don't know.'

'You mean you've never thought about it? Never discussed it with your wife?'

'We've talked about where the money comes from, but beyond that, not really. As far as she's concerned, I just do the job, get the money and help pay the bills.'

'Well, you can always think about it now. What do you reckon you'd do?'

'I guess it would depend. I'd look for spiritual guidance– '

'–at the bottom of a bottle–'

'–No, not at all. It's not something I think about very much. I prefer to leave God to His will and go about my job the best I can.'

'Cute. But you must have a backup plan. It's a tough, high stakes world out there.'

'Do you, though? Does an accountant have a backup plan? Does a farmer have a backup plan? A teacher? A doctor?'

'Some of them probably do. Some of those are stable professions, but it doesn't take much and we're cactus as far as the Force is concerned.'

'Then there's the pension to fall back on.'

'Yeah, but it's not much. You have three kids, right?'

'Yep.'

'Bet you'd struggle to feed their hungry mouths on a disability stipend.'

'My wife works, though, and she could work more. I know you think I'm crazy, but it's really not an issue for us. I don't believe you can live your life worrying about every eventuality.'

'Not even the major ones?'

'Of course, I think of some of them.'

'Mate, I strongly recommend having a think about it sometime. We're none of us getting any younger and this is a stressful fucking job at the best of times. Strewth, I feel burnt out and I'm not even forty.'

'Keep worrying about things and you'll feel twice that age before you know it.'

'I don't know what's in the water out your way or what you've been smoking, but I wouldn't mind some.'

'There's plenty to go around, mate. You're welcome anytime.'

Somehow, Owens had a feeling that offer would never be taken up. The light-hearted, yet poignant, repartee did, however, shake him from the momentary funk of sullenness. As much as they teased and goaded, he felt as close to these people as he did to anyone. They understood what others could never comprehend, and where differences lay, they commingled at the source. It was the closest he'd ever been to membership of a gang.

Owens called home that night and left a rote message after the tone.

- CHAPTER 18 -

Adrift on a sea melded brown and bottle green, Luke verbalised his introspection. Bereft of company for weeks on end, the sound of thoughts bouncing in his brain had attained a lofty magic. It regulated the flow of his Romany transfusion and sparkled with diversion when all else seemed so grave. More than providing solutions, giving voice to these thoughts broke the grip of solitude and alleviated tremors of anguish. If they were the ravings of a lunatic in despair, they were also the means by which he could consider himself sane. As his mind spun like a carousel malfunctioned, this gave him something to hang onto. To hear the certainty in his rounded vowels and the clipped precision of consonants drawn was to feel such magic reach the realms of the transcendent. Words faded in the trickery of greater meaning.

The boon of acceptance couldn't silence reflection, nor appease disquiet about the road ahead. He talked himself through this course he had taken, from the seed first sown to the boles erect before him. He considered taking notes, documenting his version of events, outlining his philosophy, pleading his case—and then thought better of it. What good would it do? What sympathy could a man with such reddened hands ever hope for, let alone expect? There could be no Jerilderie letter, no explanatory manifesto, and that was slightly painful to know. That ship had not only sailed but dispensed with its anchor. His one-page missive in homestead scribble would receive no sequel—not yet, at least. If he was to write, it would be for himself, to sift conflicting points of view and arrange them in cogent order, yet for the time it would take (and the gnash of winter on resting bones–pneumonia once was bad enough, but a return performance could signal the end) a vocal conveyance would suffice. He knew full well how his account would be received. He would remain a son of this land, and he would remain, in the eyes of this world, a cur of the cruellest kind.

As Luke was debating the virtues of each decision made, he queried why he'd never sought to bring others on board. It had crossed his mind in formative stages, and he idealised the tightknit, resourceful mateship of those star-crossed bands of misfits. The pitfalls took a backseat as he speculated what he could have achieved and the shared thrill of life on a razor's edge. In some ways, it made such sense. Inspiration had never lacked, but the cajoling and one-upmanship of like-minded souls could have spurred him to greater heights. Then there was the advantage of strength in numbers. They could have held the sun to ransom, should they have been so bold. They could have whipped a storm of fateful frenzy. They could have stood side by side to fight. Luke's gaze scanned the surrounding landscape, willing the wind to deliver his flock, but they never came. Recondite in the ways of brotherhood, the tricks of leadership and charisma's spark were not in his armoury. All he had was an insular dream and a well to fall deeper within. He would be on his own until the end.

Supplies had whittled down, and nature gave up less than its covenant. His withering guts ached in neglect. An ankle, sprained in his tired steps, flared when rested and threatened collapse when asked to bear weight. The merest sneeze hinted at a pulmonary crisis. He could engage in self-discourse all he liked, but he couldn't convince himself back to strength, fitness or health. At least he had water and shelter of a kind. One afternoon, with hunger pangs wracking and no longer worried about drawing attention, he aimed a desperate, palsied shot at a lyrebird in plume. As he picked that night at a tin of cold spaghetti, the wretchedness of his misfortune came home to roost. He was alone but lost for solitude, in nature but starved of rest.

He was perpetually on edge. The sky patrol continued at intervals unknowable; at other times every rustle of leaf-litter, avian warble or sound to snap his circuitous reverie was ripe with resignation. This forest maddened with its din. It came to mind that if he could somehow ride this out and outlast the baying masses, he would lick his wounds in silence and pledge virtue overall. He'd be no trouble to anyone. He'd right his litany of wrongs. Anything for a quiet life in the hills by a lake or burbling trickle. He could keep stock, or chickens, and learn the secrets of the earth, harvesting crops of carrots, pumpkin, corn, tubers, herbs and berries. He'd share any surplus, devoid of fear or favour, as he'd shared his boon with tipplers at the dusty western pub. And he would follow traditional methods, as some habits weren't born to die. It all seemed so simple and to speak it made it real, yet it was also intangible and agonisingly out of reach. He'd come into life full of options and hope. Now the options were odious and hope a mirage.

Though he was yet to feel the bloodhounds' breath, he was desperately worn from the chase. It had ground him into submission, and he wavered in purpose. He knew what he was running from, but where was he running to? The mere act no longer seemed enough. It was enough at the start: it was everything at the start, but every step, each subservient lunge, took that further away. Where could he go? This wilderness could not protect him forever. Without a map, he was blind to its full extent, but all worldly design has its strictures. As surely as they were coming from behind, they were bound to be approaching from other sides. For all he knew, he could be running into a bear trap. If he wasn't, if he walked unmolested out the other side, could he really slip back into society? He had very little money, scant possessions, no loyalists waiting to harbour and restore. Even if unlatched and tantalisingly ajar, the door to his parents' home could never creak open again. As so often in this abject life, all he had on which to feast was the stringy meat of hiraeth. He could abjure his wickedness and turn every leaf in this sprawling, oppressive, unbreachable bushland, but he would forever be a pariah.

Luke broke from his perambulations. He removed his pack, taking care not to disturb still-loaded pistols. He set it down with weakening hands and slumped to a moss-covered rock. He closed his eyes to shut out the noise, the staccato rhythms of the voices within. He breathed in and out, taking air like a pulley, one way then the other with monotonous flow. As thoughts came sniping, he willed them away, like swatting blowflies in an outback dunny. They were relentless. Gradually, however, the frequency eased. The strain in his haggard face relaxed by degrees. His mind became a cavity for fresh cerebration. By the time he stared at the world anew, the voices were whispered compulsion.

- CHAPTER 19 -

Like a war cabinet crafting a nation's deliverance, the searchers and their superiors conferred under ominous skies. Blaring over speaker phone, the truculent Area Commander held court.

'You realise how much grief they're giving me at HQ about this? Not blaming you lot, but it's not fucking pleasant, let me tell you. I thought we had him cornered in this place?'

'We did. We do,' responded Owens, 'it's just taking longer than hoped. By our reckoning though, he can't go much further until either we or one of the other groups catches up with him.'

'How much longer do you reckon he has?'

'Well, we don't know precisely where he is, but I would think he'll cross paths with a search party in the next twenty-four hours. And that's assuming he's moving and not staying still. If he's set up camp somewhere, I doubt we're very far behind.'

'Well, get a move on. All of you!'

'Trust me, we're going as fast as we can. We covered twenty-five k's yesterday.'

'I could cover that in my sleep. You're certain he's in there? He hasn't thrown us a red herring?'

'I'd be surprised. The car, the shoe print... Yes, he could have turned back before we started the hunt, but then you'd think he would have been seen elsewhere.'

'Yeah, the area is swarming with cops. I still can't believe they've found nothing from above.'

'It's pretty dense in here. I'd say he's well camouflaged with his dark clothes.'

'Silent bloody choppers would be nice.'

'Good luck with that.'

'So, what do you propose? More resources or just more time?'

'I think we stay the course. We're holding up okay and the supplies are lasting. If we don't have him in the next day or two then we re-evaluate the situation.'

'Alright. I fucken hope you're right, mate. The longer this goes on, the more it threatens to fade into memory of the public. I'll fight tooth and nail to ensure that doesn't happen, but we need to act quickly. I want this arsehole to suffer the full force of the law for what he's done.'

'You and me both.'

The tempo increased, if not quite to the desired standard. 'Like to see that old bitch do better' was a typical grumble. 'Hide a burger in the bush and I reckon she might' was a standard rejoinder. Regardless, struggles shared have the propensity to bind, and spirits like fog soon lifted.

There was no false optimism croaking in Owens' voice; he'd bought extra time but believed it superfluous. There's only so far that a man can run before he circles back to the point of inception. He may have overstated how well the team was travelling, but he was loath to relinquish his place in the chase. Walls were closing from all points of the compass; the wilds were shrinking, the future contracting and the recent past bleeding through. Perhaps it was more than a matter of time, but when patience held fast and senses were keen, there was little left to consider. A sense of clinical inexorability was taking hold.

Owens' phone vibrated, peremptory and bold. He fished it out of his pocket. It was his wife.

'Hi.'

'Hi.'

'How are you doing?'

'Good.'

'Just good?'

'Yeah, good.'

'How's the search going?'

'Not bad.'

'That doesn't tell me much.'

'We haven't found him yet, but I don't think we're far.'

'That's good. And you'll be home soon after that?'

'Yeah. Depends on what needs to be done here, but it should only be a matter of days.'

'That's good. I miss you, and the kids won't let on, but I think they do too.'

'Yeah. I'd better go, but I'll be in touch.'

The cop returned his phone and continued to march. A colleague looked across, smiling obliquely.

'Was that the missus?'

'Yeah.'

'Jeez, you can smell the romance there.'

'What's that about? She just called to say g'day.'

'Sure, but how long since you've seen her? There wasn't anything more to say?'

'Not really, mate, she doesn't really do small talk.'

'Or big talk either, by the sounds of it.'

'I'll call her back later. She won't mind.'

'Sure, she won't.'

'Hey, Steve,' came a voice from in front, 'there's a spare room at my place. I'll get it made up for you, mate.'

- CHAPTER 20 -

The story goes that Frank Gardiner, Prince of the Tobymen, under trammelling heat in the Golden West, pulled up stumps and with Kitty Walsh in tow, sought anonymity in dusty Apis Creek. When luck ran out and past sins caught up, he dodged the hangman and endured his time, before accepting the mercy of lawless exile. Luke knew the tale and its protagonist like the back of his hand. It loomed overhead, a sidereal keepsake, drawing a line between fancy and fact. Did Apis Creek even exist, or was it a figment, like everything else? Or could he, by virtue of youth and good character, follow Gardiner into graceful expulsion? A man who was mentor to a coterie of thieves, by the flash of his grin, the skin of his teeth and the largesse of fortune may have proffered absolution. A criminal for most, if not all, of his days, he may also have dealt in false hope.

The re-trodden path was springy and responsive under foot. At odds with the terrain, its traveller padded half-somnolent in dolorous procession, head bowed and rueful. The funerary bell rang out plangent, hypnotic. Somewhere, in abstruse mid-distance, last rites were muttered, condemning one body, expurgating a soul. Soon, in fading obsequy and preternatural hunger, the earth would devour its own.

He listened to the songs of birds on the wind. He recognised more now than he did a week ago, and that pleased him. In a complicated world, simple pleasures count for a lot, and these melodious strains, while intricately structured, seemed the simplest, purest joy of all. They jangled in chorus, enriching the forest with vibrancy spun from an earlier time. It was enough to entice a mimicry that scuppered inhibition and gave rise to new strands of hope, hinting that doomsayers had gone off too soon. More than anything else, it encouraged acceptance of what lay ahead. This was a melody that linked the ages, from indigenous gatherers and firestorm raiders, through shipwrecked waifs on nethermost shores, to colonial chest-thumpers, browbeaters, death-cheaters and into a future untold and unknown. Perhaps a note here and there had warped with time, or a coquettish female had triggered evolution, but there was constancy here and it fostered a bud of perspective.

Sun filtered through the canopy, and tensions continued to abate. He had relieved himself of some heavier items in his pack, and the reduced load made progress more like a logger's conveyor-belt than a slog through the undergrowth. He tucked into remaining supplies: dented tins of oysters built for endurance rather than flavour; a packet of noodles parched as the Simpson Desert; a chocolate bar unopened until all better options were gone. He returned empty tins to clank and clatter in his rucksack, as though the litter of products spent was worse than that of those unused. Then again, perhaps it was merely the habitual force of a young man well steeped in manners. The skin may have bruised to an obsidian sludge, but the core was far from rotten.

Thoughts were relatively clear and uncluttered. The need to externalise had drifted away, shed like a worn coat. He remembered his youth, the years of flux when every act was dynamite and every word a match. He recalled the awkwardness, the longing to fit in, the pangs of rejection and the waves of burning shame. These were overarching feelings, more than pin-point moments in time, and while he knew he held no sole dominion, they were powerful memories of a gauche larval phase. 'Why is this coming back to me now?' he wondered, but deep within it made perfect sense. He was clearing the decks, mentally and emotionally. His mind was engaged in catharsis, and in lifelong self-absorption there was nowhere to turn but within.

He harked back to the stories his uncle narrated and held tight the magic of those deeds of derring-do. The tone of that voice, deep and commanding, had tempted the words from yellowing pages, playing the piper to unforeseen doom. It spread a treacly warmth within him at the mere recollection. Had those tales enriched a life bereft, or had they run rampant under lax supervision? If he'd known what lay in store, would he have struggled against it? Or was this his fate, an unbidden, unconscious purpose of being? It had felt so at the time— had always felt so, in fact. To hear those words was to feel predestined, to feel as though he'd been born to this role, to act as the conduit he'd claimed to be. To remember his uncle's tales now was to touch on the same. And yet, as they drifted on the breeze to a magpie's tune, there was nothing left but an empty husk and questions where no answer ever came.

He soldiered on, sticking to the clearest path, cheered by each flash of recognition. He felt closer to nature than ever, as though he could almost move the trees himself, to sway them at the ebb and flow of his will. Knowledge may be power, but release carries its own substantial clout. The air seemed milder, more humid than before, yet also less oppressive, less mired in the pneumatic quagmire. It was pliable to breath, even if the trunks of mountain ash were not, and he took great quaffs into an engine building steam. Expectation was now so firmly wedged within that it ceased to fray nerve-endings, as much a part of his being as the knuckles that crowned each hand. And just as he felt no need to clench or raise a fist, a fear of what was imminent held nothing anymore. To misquote his master, he might as well have the blame as the game.

- CHAPTER 21 -

It was rising mid-morning when the band of searchers rounded a bend and began a gentle decline into the verdancy below. Owens had separated slightly from the rest of the party, if not lost in thought then at least misplaced. He was yearning for the comforts of home and the deep familiarity of that plain beyond the range. He missed his wife's cooking and the scent of her skin and wondered if he'd truly noticed these things before. He thought of his kids, an impenetrable mixture of action and ice, growing in secret like a miser's hoard, tasting the world as mute Bacchanalians, driving him crazy but never away. He missed them too and knew he had done so for some time. Not that he'd been much good at showing them. He shuddered as a chill raced down his spine, the tang of sour mash like vomit at the back of his gullet. Never again. This time, he promised himself; he meant it.

Dew sat like glow-worms on lanceolate leaves, and as sunbeams struck, they dazzled with illusion. Captivated by the play of light, it was difficult to discern manifestation from mirage. It was only when a patch of umber, subtly out of place on a quilt of greys and greens, shifted vaguely, that his gaze followed, his antennae atwitch. Under lead-weight breath he brought the caravan to a halt. He shifted into a crouch as his hand slid down in one movement, hazel oculi never leaving their target. The barrel raised. He cushioned it carefully, tracking the shape as it became a vessel of flesh. The man would have been fifty metres away, if that. And he was drawing nearer. Owens gasped. 'Check his hands, check his hands,' but they were casually by his side. He could take a shot now and end it forever. End the hunt, end the case, end this unholy charade. He could take this one down and lapels would fill with the banners of glory. He was almost on ceremony, accepting plaudits, when spectral gaze swung steadily to rendezvous with his. At the moment's shock, he almost choked on his words.

'Stop right there!'

He did. Everything did.

'Remove all weapons and put your hands on your head.'

'I'm unarmed.'

'Prove it. Empty your pockets and remove your clothing, one piece at a time.'

Even at a distance, the respondent seemed perplexed, before breaking into a wry smile.

'I thought I'd be wanted for murder, not a striptease.'

'Just do it. Slowly,' deadpanned the senior sergeant, and as an afterthought, 'nothing seductive.'

Like a gender-morphed, antipodean Artemis at sacred vestal spring, he cast his clothes one by one to the waiting forest floor.

'That's enough. We don't need to see your pecker.'

He removed his undergarments all the same.

'Don't want you to be in any doubt.'

'Okay. Now push the clothes away. Put your hands to the back of your head and drop to your knees.'

There was no resistance.

The naked man, all ribcage and collarbone, thickets of hair not a match for his shame, knelt in ultimate, utter submission and spat like a mule into the dust. If this was defiance, it was unusually drawn. As Owens edged forward, he could see goose bumps puckering the expanse of calcite, concave skin. When he stood a body-length from this wreck of humanity, he towered like a priest over baptismal subjugation.

'Luke Anthony Barclay, you are under arrest for double murder.'

(He was dying to add, 'And other acts of wanton criminal bastardry', but he checked his temper and kept to the script.)

'You have the right to remain silent and the right to a lawyer. Do you understand?'

'Yeah. And the right to put my clothes back on?'

'We'll help you with that.'

They led him away, shackled and ragged, through oil-paint opacity epic and bleak. They took no chances, no liberties shared save bestowal of air and a pulse. Distended in gloat, they inched through the landscape, a camel train traded in dunes for digression. The presiding mood was one of buoyancy, under towed by a current of hubristic relief. To have emerged empty handed would have been unforgiveable. To offer a corpse would have been a kiss without a cause. In a world seeking answers and meaning above all, they'd deliver an exemplar of exquisite surrogation.

Owens chewed his words for some time before breaking the silence.

'I have to say, I expected a fight.'

'Sorry. I'm spent.'

'Yep, you surely are.'

After a moment's thought, Owens continued.

'Why did you do it? Good upbringing, loving parents, decent schooling: what possessed you to throw it all away?'

'You wouldn't understand.'

'Not if you don't tell me.'

They continued in quietude and morose disconnect.

Beyond the yawning chasm of words unspoken, the captor probed again.

'What would your parents think? I met them–beautiful, gentle people. They're distraught.'

'I'm not for them to worry about.'

'That's bullshit. You're everything for them to worry about. Their only son and heir.'

Luke turned his head and glared at his interrogator. Watery eyes and a quavering voice betrayed the tough guy affectations.

'Guess their luck's out then.'

Owens wanted to punch him.

Further along the scabrous path, the older man gave air to grievance.

'You think yourself some kind of bushranger, don't you?'

No response.

'You realise they were common criminals: no more, no less?'

'You realise you know less than you think?'

'Tell me then. Explain to me the virtues of these heroes of yours. I'm all ears. It's not as though I'm going anywhere in a hurry.'

'You wouldn't understand.'

'For fuck's sake! You've ruined lives across the state and won't even explain why?'

The younger man shook non-existent flies from his face.

Incensed, Owens felt his tether fray.

'I will see to it,' he explained through teeth like a fox-trap, 'that the full force of the law comes down on you. And when it does, I will be there watching, staring you down as you plummet to Hell.'

'Not if I don't take you there first.'

Impulse overrode instinct, and a jab shook the midriff of the manacled intransigent. He was momentarily winded but otherwise unswayed. A ribbon of spittle passed from lip to chin. And then a smile, first sheepish, then increasingly defiant, cutlassed his sunken features. Enraged and unhinging, the cop struck again. By the time he was done, restrained by colleagues, inchoate ruptures of indigo and violet, specked alabaster like a star-pricked night sky, were mottling a torso bent double but splinted by knowledge new-formed and unshakeably dire.

Between scraggy, rasping breaths, the victim found voice.

'I may have problems, but what about you?'

The mocking tone flipped axis. 'With me? Ha, you wouldn't understand.'

What Owens thought had been a whisper had in fact been broadcast wide. His colleagues looked on, eyes agape, until one spoke up in concern.

'Mate, you okay? Hitting a prisoner is not a good look in this day and age.'

'I'm fine. He just got to me, that's all.'

'You're not wrong there. You alright to keep going?'

'I am fine.'

Against better judgment, the troupe kept no distance between combatants as it carried on through man-made haze.

They reached a pre-determined point after noon had crested and then waited for the liberating harness to drop. They passed time snacking from zip-bags of scroggin, smoking cigarettes to ash and sketching plans for a drink to unwind at journey's end. Owens sat aloof, hand club-like then flexing, upbraiding himself for his loss of restraint. With time, he felt he'd understand his motivation. Harder to reconcile would be why it had felt so bloody good. He thought he knew what kind of man he was, yet in this winter of scrabbling discontent one tenement seemed to shake after another. Something was off, but he couldn't quite put his finger on it. In the absence of time, he offered repentance that only a lip reader or soul-stealer might hope to deduce. Non-corporeal fine print could be dealt with later.

Hovering like a dragonfly of mutant proportion, they heard salvation long before it caught sight. Upper branches crooked from buffeting gusts and roiling air rappelled down trembling trunks to the open space below. Lawmen gawked as a force beyond their remit assumed position to carry them away. Then, as blurring rotors side-slashed the sky, a door opened, and thumbs up signalled the coming descent. They looked on as coils swung down and straightened into rope, suspended taut yet gently lolling. At the end of the pendulous cable—vaguely umbilical and thrumming with life—a rescue cradle hung like a teardrop from its lachrymose filament.

On trepidant thermals this din took form, and relegated instruction to gesture and might. For those who yelled, it was energy wasted. Footsore and surly, the prisoner was escorted towards the waiting strop. After some discussion, they had decided that Owens would remain his protector and that some things are best left to moulder on the distant forest floor. A gale of man's creation made the going tough, but the team ensured that man and his minder were strapped in and secured. And then like figures from a platonic Kama Sutra, they rose, eyes averted, in lust-less embrace. As ground gave way, they were winched with caution past bark-skinned columns and then brushed by gum leaves like a riding whip's kiss. The prisoner's coat became a crinoline framework, fanned by an updraught indecent and cold. Owens felt the kicking of a leg and looked to see a captive as glum as before.

'Not long now,' he bellowed, fighting the racket of confluent sounds.

His tandem stared blankly.

They were hoisted higher until all trees could see their hindquarters and the strewn arras of Australian bush was an ocean that lapped the spherical rim. Owens convinced himself he could see halfway home. He convinced himself that everything was fine and that he'd slip like a cat-burglar back into regular existence. He swore he was in control, because he was a man and that was his calling. Any lapse had been just that: a lapse. Back on his patch, smoke funnelling the chimney bricks, dinner warm on the table, work talk strictly forbidden, he'd be himself again.

It all happened suddenly and seemed to be over in an instant, though it doubtless took closer to two or three. Those below, when placed under oath, swore to nothing more than specks contorting like bacteria under a lens. Those above, not twenty feet shy and hauling ever nearer, wished they'd paid more attention. To them, it had seemed a case of vertigo swollen by personal strain. In the tumult and uproar, bounds of extremity muddied; not knowing what to look for, they had in fact seen nothing. It would be for crumbling bones in years to come to ache at the pain of remembrance.

At the dead-end of the wire, retracting like a lizard's tongue but in no way built for speed, languid ascent turned sinister. Somehow, with hands fettered and feet nearer cloud than soil, the convict had deftly loosened and then unclasped straps, like some aerial contortionist, shape-shifting and wriggling free until he sat like a child on a playground swing. Unhitched at the maws of fathomless void, he drank stunned realisation from the face of his erstwhile adversary. He watched as panic took hold and life in all its feverish assuredness cat-fought and strove. Like an off-guard combatant the tide was against, but flesh takes time to weaken. It was when gainsaid the chafing of straps on legs that panic ramped to breaking point. Owens thrust his hands to snag them in something, anything stable that might keep him bound, while clutching at clips to re-harness mid-air. Yet for all the urgency he was losing ground. Each frantic effort met a parrying blow. Each latch that clicked was soon broken. The rancid breath and death's head bearing down was becoming too much to resist.

The bushranger snarled and if his words were heard, it was barely as a whisper.

'As my fate goes, so does yours.'

Summoned of ultimate, volcanic reserves of strength, he grabbed an arm, yanked and twisted until shoulder ripped from socket and then felt the agonised mass behind it follow into the ether. The wire quit its reeling. The harness flapped in the wind.

Deprived of all recourse for upward impetus, their splayed bodies like Devil's playthings freefell towards the echidna spine of green-tipped wood beneath. And like molluscs taken as seabird's catch and dashed for fleshy presentment, they met the earth with a graceless thud, shells cracked and innards seeping.

- CHAPTER 22 -

They converged from all angles, in shock and at speed. As bodies tripped over knotted roots and were scratched by twigs and bark, minds remained voids of silence deaf to chaos, blind to strife. Hearts that kept a gentle beat were now thumping, pulsing oxygen like mad things in a frenzy. An overriding weight of disbelief hung burdensome and prone. Paths to destiny had eroded in plain sight, like the careful trails from British ports that fanned southbound transportation. The world was dawning crimson and cold in a glut of turmoil's cunning, where the harrowed lot of those within would bow to buckle. First on the scene checked for a pulse and for signs of cognition. In a motion of almost fluid despair, his reaction compelled no translation. Colleagues stopped in their tracks. Shoulders dropped. Disbelief took on a bleaker tone, wringing winter dry of despondence. The second body was almost an afterthought, a cruel inconvenience.

For now, they left the bodies where they lay. Blankets covered their aberrant forms, but all knew the damage was done. When procedure swung low with ropes unfurled and finally bade farewell to this godforsaken forest, relief could barely draw breath for the overtones of sadness and shock. Consolation would come in many forms, but for now there was laconic reassurance. Fate had played a wicked game.

News spread like the fires that ravaged this land from a point in time long forgotten, blazing misery through blistered skin to rest in the chill of cracked and brittle bone. They sought answers where questions found it hard to tread, and as they settled, they opened as many doors as they closed. Some would remain ajar forever. Dreams had turned mute, yet with the fullness of time they would again find a voice. Perspective shifted and broadened its scope, deepened by grief and reflection. Episodic obscurity became a single, tangible, horrific mass, from a series of events to a consolidated act. The culprit became a caricature, the soulless shadow of a man out of time. To the victims, no solace, no rightful resurrection: only dignity, sorrow and respect.

The plains past the Range stretch beyond the far horizon. Sorrel-hued and scarred by gales, their patchwork fields spread like waves of colonisation doomed to always bear their impression. Within this land lies deepest time, spanned vast and unexplainable. This is a realm of man, of woman, of child, of primeval forces and cogs turned within. As the cogs rotate, so do the sting of grief and the rapture of joy filter through memory to dust. Emotions recede. Lives, battered and bruised and resilient beyond measure, evolve and expand out of sight. In these sweeping plains there is harbourage and grounding.

High on a loft of vaulted rock, a solitary figure in silhouette watches over.

- EPILOGUE -

'Let me tell you a story of bushrangers bold, of bolters and renegades, colonial spectres, currency lads and convicts at arms. Listen close, but keep the magic in check, leave those tales to an era behind us. Think of these men and the women beside them, admire their pluck and their will to survive. Yes, gasp at their exploits, the wild inhibition, the fist in the face of a mercurial foe, but think of the time, of the place, of the setting a frontier settlement finding its feet. Consider their adversaries, men and women just the same, by fortune or favour pitched in life's higher circles. Villains of the peace, through the florid lens of lore—for a people seeking heroes always need an adversary. They were game in their own way, on their side of the law. Listen to my tale, but take a step back, and give the full picture a chance to unfold. Context is the key, my boy, and within its arms does compassion lie. And as my story closes, keep imagination fierce, yearn for the old days—by all means yearn deeply—but pay them the courtesy which they are due. For those who lived, who fought, who died, who struggled to find their way through the haze, that's the very least they deserve.'

Shawline Publishing Group Pty Ltd

www.shawlinepublishing.com.au

SHAWLINE
PUBLISHING
GROUP